"You're...you're flirting with me?"

Elizabeth backed up two steps, sure her eyes had gone wide and stupid.

"Do you mind?"

She felt her head moving from side to side. Had this man, this absolutely drop-dead-handsome man, just agreed that he was flirting with her? Her, Elizabeth Carstairs, better known as *Mom?* Her? "Uh...no?"

They exchanged smiles, Elizabeth lost in the moment, somewhere she hadn't been in too many years to recall....

D0210110

Dear Reader,

In high school I worked as a bridal consultant in an upscale women's clothing store. Then my boss went on leave of absence and I became the seventeen-year-old in charge of the entire bridal salon for one crazy summer. And I fell in love with everything to do with brides and happily-ever-afters.

There is nothing like the special glow that comes over a bride when she puts on that perfect gown. But why should that special glow be reserved for first-time brides? That's why I created SECOND-CHANCE BRIDAL and Chessie Burton, a young woman who has devoted herself to second chances.

Come along as Chessie and her friends meet Elizabeth Carstairs, a prospective second-time-around bride who is far from sure about taking another trip down the aisle. How fortunate that she chose the right bridal salon.

I'm having a blast writing the books that make up this series, and I hope you'll have a blast reading them. Oh, and I hope you'll like the gowns I—that is, *Chessie*—picked out for her brides.

Kasey Michaels

SUDDENLY A
BRIDE

KASEY MICHAELS

Silhouette®

SPECIAL EDITION®

Published by Silhouette Books

America's Publisher of Contemporary Romance

If you purchased this book without a cover you should be aware that this book is stolen property. It was reported as "unsold and destroyed" to the publisher, and neither the author nor the publisher has received any payment for this "stripped book."

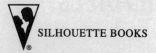 SILHOUETTE BOOKS

ISBN-13: 978-0-373-65517-5

SUDDENLY A BRIDE

Recycling programs
for this product may
not exist in your area.

Copyright © 2010 by Kathryn Seidick

All rights reserved. Except for use in any review, the reproduction or utilization of this work in whole or in part in any form by any electronic, mechanical or other means, now known or hereafter invented, including xerography, photocopying and recording, or in any information storage or retrieval system, is forbidden without the written permission of the editorial office, Silhouette Books, 233 Broadway, New York, NY 10279 U.S.A.

This is a work of fiction. Names, characters, places and incidents are either the product of the author's imagination or are used fictitiously, and any resemblance to actual persons, living or dead, business establishments, events or locales is entirely coincidental.

This edition published by arrangement with Harlequin Books S.A.

For questions and comments about the quality of this book please contact us at Customer_eCare@Harlequin.ca.

® and TM are trademarks of Harlequin Books S.A., used under license. Trademarks indicated with ® are registered in the United States Patent and Trademark Office, the Canadian Trade Marks Office and in other countries.

Visit Silhouette Books at www.eHarlequin.com

Printed in U.S.A.

Books by Kasey Michaels

Silhouette Special Edition

**Suddenly a Bride #2035

Silhouette Desire
The Tycoon's Secret #1910

HQN Books

*How to Tame a Lady
*How to Tempt a Duke
†Mischief 24/7
†Mischief Becomes Her
†Dial M for Mischief
††Becket's Last Stand
††Return of the Prodigal
††A Reckless Beauty
††A Most Unsuitable Groom
††Beware of Virtuous Women
††The Dangerous Debutante
††A Gentleman by Any Other Name*

**Second-Chance Bridal
*The Daughtry Family
†The Sunshine Girls
††The Beckets of Romney Marsh

KASEY MICHAELS

is a *USA TODAY* bestselling author of more than one hundred books. She has earned three starred reviews from *Publishers Weekly,* and has won a RITA® Award from Romance Writers of America, an *RT Book Reviews* Career Achievement Award, Waldenbooks and Bookrak awards and several other commendations for her writing excellence in both contemporary and historical novels. Kasey resides in Pennsylvania with her family, where she is always at work on her next book.

Readers may contact Kasey via her Web site, KaseyMichaels.com.

To Gail Chasan,
for allowing me the pleasure of writing this series.

Chapter One

Prospective bank robbers probably cased the joint less thoroughly. Elizabeth Carstairs had driven down Chestnut Street in her five-year-old compact SUV at least six times in the past week—and three times in the past hour.

Down Chestnut, right on Sixth, right on Maple, right on Seventh, right on Chestnut. She had been going in squares rather than circles but getting just as dizzy. And each time, she slowed the car as she passed the old, Victorian three-story, painted a whimsical shade of violet with darker violet and green trim. A beautifully restored painted lady, as Elizabeth had heard such houses called, set back from the street and surrounded by clever shrubbery that drew the eye toward the house and the painted sign on the front lawn.

Second Chance Bridal. And, beneath that intriguing name, in flowing script, this further explanation: *Because sometimes two (or three) is the charm.*

Elizabeth now stood on the sidewalk in front of the house, having finally parked her car a block away when she'd at last convinced herself she was being an idiot. She stared at the herringbone-design gray brick walkway that led to the covered wraparound porch and the double doors set between matching bay windows displaying gowns on headless mannequins.

A bridal shop. That's all it was. People went inside bridal salons all the time. Looked around. Didn't always buy something. Although it was probably a foregone conclusion that the person was there to buy, because the person wouldn't be looking at bridal gowns unless she was getting married. It wasn't like bridal salons also sold jeans and underwear or something. If you went inside a bridal salon, it could pretty well be determined that you were there because you were going to get married. And if the salon you entered was named Second Chance Bridal, it was also reasonably certain that you weren't exactly new to the process. Still, walking into a bridal salon was like being committed to the thing. Or, as Elizabeth was beginning to wonder about herself, like she *should be* committed.

No. She couldn't do it. The part of her that wanted to do it was hiding somewhere while the part of her that was scared spitless was standing front and center, feet itching to move back down the block, to the car, to escape.

"Hi there. I'm late, aren't I?"

Elizabeth turned toward the sound of the voice. A bouncy, bright-eyed woman of about thirty, her head a mop of wonderfully casual, light copper curls that all ended bluntly at chin level, was heading toward her, a wide smile on her face.

"Excuse me?" Elizabeth asked, tempted to look behind her, hoping the woman was talking to someone else.

The redhead was digging in her oversize shoulder bag now, obviously on the hunt for something. "I always think I'll have enough time for lunch and at least one errand, and I'm always wrong. I should have known there'd be a line at the dry cleaners. Ten dollars for two measly blouses? *Two*. Remember when everything was wash-and-wear? No muss, no fuss? Whatever happened to those days?"

Elizabeth only nodded, agreeing with the sentiment. She'd found herself ironing everything again when, for years, she'd pretty much used her steam iron as a doorstop. Now everything seemed to come out of the dryer in wrinkled clumps, especially the boys' shirts.

The woman pulled a set of keys out of her bag, along with a cell phone that she flipped open and then grimaced at, wrinkling her pert nose. "I stopped wearing a watch, thinking I could just see the time on my phone, you know? Very hip, very modern. I probably should have stuck with the watch. Yup, late. Nearly five minutes late."

Because she was naturally polite, and because she

thought it might be time she tried to say something, Elizabeth said, "Oh, but—"

Which was as far as she got before the bouncy redhead held out her hand, leaving Elizabeth no choice but to take it.

"Hi, I'm Chessie Burton. And you must be my two o'clock. What do you say we get out of this hot sun?"

"I, um, I…" Elizabeth couldn't seem to get past Chessie's beautiful, open, smiling face and velvet steamroller charm. "Yes, sure. It is hot, isn't it?"

"For this early in June, yes. I think so," Chessie said, leading the way up the gray brick path—or The Last Mile, as Elizabeth had been thinking of it. "But that's the beauty of Pennsylvania, don't you think? We get all four seasons. I couldn't imagine living with such heat year-round—or never getting to see the trees turn colors in the fall. Of course, after the first snowfall I always think I've seen enough, thank you, and begin hoping for spring. Ah, here we go."

Chessie had inserted one of the keys from her ring into the big brass lock and pushed open the old-fashioned door. An air-conditioned breeze rushed out at them, and Elizabeth hastened inside, drawn by both the coolness and the sweet smell of fresh cut flowers.

While Chessie flipped the sign in the front window from Closed to Open, Elizabeth looked around the high-ceilinged room made welcoming by the clever arrangement of chairs and tables that spoke more of a fancy parlor than a place of business.

"What a pretty room," she said, pretending not to notice the glass cases displaying gloves and headpieces and ring-bearer pillows and pretty white leather-covered books with words like *Our Wedding* stamped on them.

"Thank you." Chessie walked to the half-circle reception desk and flipped open an appointment book. "Hmm, that's funny. I don't have a two o'clock anymore. Eve marked it as canceled." She looked at Elizabeth. "Good Lord, don't tell me I just kidnapped you off the street."

Maybe it was the beautiful building. Maybe it was at last being inside it rather than circling the place like some loon. Or maybe it was the comically horrified look on Chessie's expressive face. Whatever it was, Elizabeth felt her nervousness melt away as she laughed softly.

"You didn't kidnap me. I was…well, I thought I might be coming inside anyway. I'm Elizabeth Carstairs, by the way. I probably should have said that earlier, but—"

"But I wouldn't let you get a word in sideways," Chessie interrupted, nodding knowingly. "Sorry about that. I could put on a fresh pot of coffee, but I make miserable coffee. Would you like a soda? Diet or regular?"

"Regular, thanks," Elizabeth told her, any lingering thoughts she might have of finding a way back out to the street now gone. "I don't have an appointment, you know."

"That's all right. Obviously, neither have I." Chessie opened a bottom door on what looked like an antique highboy chest but somehow housed a small refrigerator below the double top doors and pulled out two cans of soda. Opening the top doors revealed neat rows of glassware and some small dessert dishes. With swift efficiency, ice was put in the glasses, sodas were popped open and poured and pretty vanilla cookies with fruity centers were arranged on one of the dessert plates.

Chessie used the plate to motion to the Queen Anne high-back chairs arranged around a low coffee table in front of a fireplace currently fronted by a large bouquet of live flowers.

"So," she said once they both were seated and Elizabeth was carefully putting her glass down on what looked to be a hand-crocheted lace coaster, "when's the wedding?"

And there it was, the big question, or at least one of them. "I don't know," Elizabeth answered honestly, and then smiled weakly. "I haven't really said yes yet."

Chessie tipped her head to one side. "And you thought maybe trying on some gowns might help you make up your mind?"

Elizabeth was genuinely surprised. "You're a mind reader?"

"No, although wouldn't that be fun? Second-timers are a more wary lot, I've found, that's all. First-timers rush in—like all fools, right? But the second time around? We tend to look a whole lot more before we leap."

"You sound as if you've got experience in that area."

"Not really. Let's say I'm still licking wounds from an *almost* first time, not that they aren't pretty well healed. My very first sale was my own never-used wedding gown." Chessie slapped her hands against her thighs and stood up. "Come on. Let's go play."

"Oh, but I don't want to waste your time," Elizabeth protested. She noticed that she was standing up and following the woman even as she was saying the words. "I'm really not here to buy."

"And I'm not here to sell. Well, that's not true, is it? I own the joint, so of course I want to sell. But I don't have any more appointments this afternoon. Only Eve has a three o'clock, and we just got several new gowns in this morning. I'm dying to see them on somebody other than myself. You're a four?"

"Uh…yes. A four. I don't think I'm wearing the right bra to be trying on gowns." Not the right bra, not the right anything, considering she was clad in a simple white tank top and a plaid skort that had probably seen better days. "And sandals. Sandals aren't quite the look, are they?"

"Mere details." Chessie opened an ornately paneled ivory wood door, its design picked out in gold, and motioned for Elizabeth to step inside a large dressing room. There was a sort of raised stage in the middle of it and several rather full half slips hung from pegs on one wall. "You'll find strapless bras in the top three drawers of that chest over there. We probably have your size. Shoes are on the shelving behind the door. I'll give you a few minutes and be back with the goodies."

Once the door was closed and Elizabeth was alone, she looked at her reflection in the three-way mirror, still not quite believing what was happening. Chessie Burton was like some friendly tidal wave washing over her, and she didn't seem to have the will to resist.

Or maybe she really wanted to try on wedding gowns?

"And how are you going to know if you don't try?" she asked her reflection. Her reflection stuck its tongue out at her.

She found a strapless push-up bra in the second drawer and quickly stripped down to put it on before sliding out of her sandals and into a pair of white backless heels that made her doubly aware that all she was wearing were the bra and her hip-hugging underpants. High heels and underwear. Now, there was a look.

Elizabeth bit her bottom lip on a giggle just as Chessie knocked on the door and then entered the room, carrying several plastic bags she held up high by their hangers. "I only brought three. It's so easy to feel overwhelmed. And only the ivory and the blush. With your fair skin and hair, I think white would just wash you out, and who needs that?"

"I've already worn white. With twin boys at home, I really don't qualify anymore, anyway."

"I doubt one first-time bride in fifty does these days. But as Eve says, if you can wait the year or more it seems to take to hire the hall and plan a wedding without ripping each other's clothes off, well, then you probably shouldn't be getting married in the first place. In fact, that should have been my first clue."

"My pregnancy test strip turned positive the morning of my wedding. I don't know if the white gown made me look pale or if it was the morning sickness," Elizabeth said, no longer blushing at the memory. "I told Jamie when my father handed me off to him at the altar."

Chessie had unzipped the first bag and paused in lifting the gown out of it. "My God, what did he do?"

Now Elizabeth did blush. "Let's just say it was a good thing we had a videographer at the ceremony, because Jamie always said he didn't remember much of anything after that. Eight months later we had the twins. It was…a busy year."

"But a happy one, I can tell. Okay, here's the first one. It's a mermaid skirt, so you're going to have to step into it. I don't think it's your style. You're more wholesome than daring, I'd say, but everyone has to try on a mermaid skirt at least once, right?"

Elizabeth eyed the gown warily. "It looks rather… formfitting."

"And you've got the form to fit it, you lucky dog. I can't believe you carried twins. How old are they?"

"Danny and Mikey? They just turned seven. We only moved here around Thanksgiving of last year, so I'm still pretty much at a loss as to what to do with them now that school is out for the summer. They keep me pretty busy and— Oh, good Lord. Is that me?"

The gown fit her like the proverbial glove. She seemed to go in at all the right places and out at some mildly impressive other places. The material was beautiful, the lace exquisite, the skirt that flared out just at her knees a marvel of engineering. And she felt like a complete fraud.

"It certainly is all you. What do you think?"

"I think I should probably leave the glamour to someone who feels more confident in pulling it off."

"Agreed. Yet you'd be surprised at how many brides feel strapless and mermaid are the only way to go these days. Have you thought about T-ball?"

Elizabeth half shimmied out of the unsuitable gown, then rested a hand on Chessie's shoulder as she carefully stepped clear of it. "Excuse me?"

"For your boys," Chessie told her as she hung up the gown once more, zipping the bag as if to say "well, that didn't work." "Baseball, you know? This entire area is very big on youth baseball. The younger kids, like your Danny and Mikey, often hit from a sort of rubber tee. T-ball, get it? Or maybe they're old enough to have real pitchers. You'd have to check."

Elizabeth crossed her arms against her bare stomach, hugging tight her insecurities, as well as memories she still had trouble facing when they slammed into her unexpectedly. "Oh. Baseball. I don't know a thing about sports. Jamie bought the twins baseball gloves and these cute little footballs while they were still in the hospital nursery. He was so excited to think about teaching his boys how to play…."

She could feel Chessie's eyes on her for a moment, but then the other woman tactfully turned back to the clear plastic bags and unzipped another one. "I think this one will be more your speed."

"Somewhere between slow and stop, huh?"

"Oh, I like you," Chessie said with a grin. "Just scrunch down for this one and lift up your arms. I'll guide you to the armholes."

Once more Elizabeth found herself almost mindlessly obeying, standing up again as she emerged from the yards and yards of tea-stained material to look at her reflection in the mirror.

"Oh, yes. I thought so," Chessie said with some satisfaction. "It's a perfect fit except for being just a little bit long. Step up on the podium so you get the full effect of the hemline."

Elizabeth did as she was told. The gown felt comfortable, like something she'd owned for years and didn't even have to think about when she was wearing it. But the way it looked, the way *she* looked…

She ran her fingertips along the modestly scooped neckline, the lovely cap sleeves that followed the cut of the scoop. She swallowed a sudden lump in her throat as her eyes traveled down the front of the gown to the simple Empire waistline, the soft A-line skirt. She turned sideways to see there was a small sweep train on the gown that was all clean lines, no frills in the cut of it. Which made the clever use of lace elegant and not fussy.

"What…what is it made of?" she asked when she could find her voice.

"Silk crepe. Comfy, isn't it? And that's alençon lace on the bodice and in those sort of appliqués on the skirt and hem. Louis the Fourteenth, I think it was, called it the queen of laces. I love it because it's so rich yet not showy. I mean, you don't need sparkles when you've got alençon—just those few pearls stitched here and there. Oh, right, pearls. Wait here a second."

Elizabeth nodded rather numbly as Chessie sped out of the room, obviously a woman on a mission, and lifted the skirt slightly at either side as she turned this way, that way, attempting to find something wrong with the gown.

But there was nothing. It was perfect. The gown had been made for her. It was *her* gown.

Her bottom lip began to tremble and she bit down on it, trying to hold on to her shredding composure.

"I remember seeing something like this in the photograph of the gown. Bend down so I can get this over your head," Chessie said as she reentered the room. The next thing Elizabeth knew she was wearing a long rope of beautiful ivory pearls Chessie had wrapped once high around her neck before the length of the rope fell over her bodice and extended an inch or two past her waist. "Perfect! Nothing on your head—as if you'd need anything with that gorgeous blond hair of yours. No gloves, no bracelets. I'd say carry two or three long-stemmed calla lilies, their stems wrapped in simple ivory silk ribbon, but that's it. Utter simplicity, complete elegance, a perfect second wedding."

Elizabeth's eyes were stinging now and she blinked quickly, doing her best to hold back the tears.

"We could try the third gown. We could try another ten gowns, twenty. But this is it, Elizabeth. You can't deny it. This is *your* gown. I knew it the minute I saw you standing on the pavement. Am I good, or what? No, don't answer that. I've got a big enough head as it is. Now let's talk about the groom."

And Elizabeth, who made it a point never to show her emotions in public, burst into tears.

Ten minutes later, with Eve and her bride now tucked away in the large dressing room, Chessie and Elizabeth were upstairs in Chessie's living quarters, facing each other from a matched set of chintz love seats divided by a glass-topped coffee table.

"Better now?" Chessie asked, tucking her legs up under her on the cushions.

Elizabeth dabbed at her eyes with the last of the several tissues she'd employed after Chessie had shoved a box of them in her face. "Better enough to feel really, *really* embarrassed, you mean? Then, yes, I'm fine. I don't know what happened down there."

Chessie pulled a face. "I do. I opened my big mouth and inserted my size-nine foot. You told me right off the top that you weren't sure you were going to say yes to the guy. Richard was it?"

"Yes, Richard. And he's the dearest man," she added quickly, hastening to defend him. "He's kind and generous and gentle and…"

"Boring?"

"No! Richard is anything but boring. The boys and I live with him, you know."

Chessie took a drink from her glass. "There's nothing

wrong with that. But, hon, your reaction downstairs? Maybe living with and marrying are two different things? I mean, fun's fun and all of that, but marriage is a pretty big commitment."

Elizabeth hastily raised her hands and waved them in front of her, as if to wipe away the last few moments of conversation. "Let me start over. I *work* for Richard. I work for him, and the boys and I live in his guesthouse. Better?"

"Definitely clearer," her new friend said, smiling. "So what sort of work do you do for the guy?"

Elizabeth was feeling more confident now, with the subject of marriage at least temporarily shelved. "Richard's a writer. He's never married, lives alone and would probably starve to death without realizing it if someone didn't take care of him. That's how it began, with me answering his ad for part-time employment. He didn't ask for skills, and since I really don't have any outside of taking care of a house and making a fairly memorable pot roast, I seemed to fit the bill. But it was clear from the outset that Richard needed more than just someone to pick up after him and prepare a few meals."

"I think I'm getting the picture. The creative genius who forgets to eat and walks around for hours with his glasses on top of his head, thinking he's lost them?"

Elizabeth smiled. "Pretty much like that, yes, when he's deep into a book. I'd thought I'd just come and go, with him not even realizing I'd been there. But often we talked about things, about his work. Within a week he'd found out I was renting an apartment with the boys, and he'd convinced me that boys need green grass to play on and their mother within earshot whenever possible. The next thing I knew I was a salaried, full-time employee, and the boys and I were installed in the rooms above his garages. They're very large garages."

"How convenient for him—that is, for all of you. Sounds like this Richard of yours is pretty wealthy. I mean, garages—plural."

"There was family money, he told me, but he's also quite successful on his own. His books are wonderful. He runs his ideas past me now, using me as a sounding board, I guess you'd say, since he used to bounce ideas off Sam The Dog—that's his dog's name—but Sam isn't a very harsh critic. As he had me take on more and more of what he calls his scut work, Richard hired a new housekeeper so that now I'm strictly his personal assistant. Except for Sunday pot roast, of course."

"Can't forget the memorable pot roast," Chessie said, lifting her soda glass in a small toast. "So what does an author's personal assistant do?"

Elizabeth knew that Chessie wanted to keep her talking, keep her mind off what had happened downstairs, and she was more than willing to go along with that idea.

"Oh, I run errands, balance his checkbook, answer a *lot* of fan mail, fight with his publicist over proposed interviews and photo shoots he never wants to do, do Internet research for him, proof his pages once he's ready for someone else to see them. And I've even come up with an idea or two for him. Richard swears he doesn't know how he ever produced a single word without me. It's…it's very exciting—especially since, as I already told you, I have no formal training of any kind. Richard says I have a natural good ear, whatever that is."

"It all sounds like a dream job. And Richard doesn't mind the boys?"

Elizabeth lowered her head slightly. "I don't think he notices them much on a day-to-day basis. But he certainly doesn't *mind* them. It's, as you'd imagine, a very large property. The boys have lunch with Richard regularly, once a week, and he asks about their schoolwork and what they want to be when they grow up—things like that. He bought them an entire array of those interactive electronic games, the complete systems with all the bells and whistles, and then gave them each new computers and flat-screen television sets for their rooms. For Christmas, he gave the three of us a week in Florida and passes to all the theme parks, even though he couldn't come with us. The twins think he's Santa Claus and Bill Gates, all tied up with a ribbon around his neck."

"Not a lot there not to love, huh?"

"No, there's not," Elizabeth agreed, once more not quite meeting Chessie's eyes. "He is…a bit older than I am."

Chessie seemed to sit up straighter, as if coming to attention. "Oh, yes? How much older? Ten years? Fifteen?"

"Seventeen." Elizabeth lifted her chin. "But that just

makes him more stable, more dependable. And…and we have so much in common."

"Yes. You both make sure Richard is well taken care of," Chessie said, and then winced. "No, I'm sorry. I didn't mean that. I don't even know the man. But I think I see where this is going. Richard has found what he thinks is his muse, and you've found a secure home and probably a pretty good future for the twins. Am I right?"

"Is there something wrong with that?"

"You tell me. I'm not the one who burst into tears downstairs."

Elizabeth buried her face in her hands. "I know, I know. But marrying Richard is so very logical." She dropped her hands into her lap and looked at Chessie. "Jamie and I married when we were halfway through college, and as I told you before, I was already pregnant with the twins. I hadn't planned to leave school, but the pregnancy changed all of that, for both of us. Jamie worked at a job he hated and went to weekend college to finish his bachelor's degree. Everything was a struggle, but that was all right, because we had the boys. We had each other. Young love, you know? And then, just when he'd found a great job and we finally were seeing the end of the student loans and formula and diaper bills, Jamie got sick."

She turned her head, her hands forming into fists she batted together as if to beat away the anger she still felt at the unfairness of it all. The anger and the loss and the terror and the cruel, twisting grief that had mentally and physically pushed her to her knees at Jamie's grave-side that last awful day. The long, sleepless nights, the responsibilities that never stopped, the loneliness that had at last turned her grief to some sort of stony acceptance.

"I'm so sorry, Elizabeth," Chessie said quietly. "So very sorry."

"So am I. We were so in love. And then we were so…tired. So stressed all the time. And just…and just when we thought we could find what we'd seemed to have lost in those diapers and bills, those constant pressures, it was all snatched away, and I felt as if my life was over. I care very much for Richard, and he cares for me. It's…it's safer."

"He knows you don't love him?"

Elizabeth pulled a fresh tissue from the box sitting on the cushion beside her. "Oh, I do love him. And he loves me. In our own way. We're very good friends. We're…compatible."

"And he's all right with that? *You're* all right with that?"

"Sometimes," Elizabeth said defensively, and then sighed. "And sometimes…well, sometimes maybe not so much."

"So what you're telling me is that you and Richard love each other—but you're not *in* love with each other? You're very good friends and compatible. Do you think people *really* can be that way? That it's *safer?* Surely somebody gets hurt, sooner or later? Somebody breaks the bargain, and falls in love for real?" Then Chessie held up her hands. "Hey, but not my problem, not my business to interfere, right? I'm sure you're doing some very heavy, sensible thinking about all of this."

"If we can call trying on wedding gowns to see what happens even the least bit sensible."

"Oh, I don't know. How did it make you feel trying on that gown?"

Elizabeth felt a ridiculous giggle prickling at the back of her throat. "Beautiful, passionate, seductive, exciting. I'd have married it tomorrow, no hesitation." Then she sighed. "But I'm no closer to knowing what I should do about Richard's proposal than I was this morning or last week."

"Then you know what, Elizabeth? Forget it for now. Tell Richard you need more time, and just…forget about it. School only let out a couple of days ago, you've got the twins home and need to do something to keep them occupied for the summer, all sorts of things to do. Am I right?"

"I only let them game, as they call it, two hours a day. They're already telling me they're bored. And, believe me, bored twins of a certain age—of any age, I'm beginning to think—can be like ticking time bombs. Yes, I need to devote some time to them. And Richard leaves in a few days for a five-city book tour and won't be home for a week. Yes, you're right. It's not like either Richard or I are in any sort of huge rush."

"Yeah, the test didn't show up positive this morning," Chessie said, grinning.

"Hardly. The only time I've been in Richard's bedroom was when I was in charge of changing the sheets. Oh, I shouldn't be saying these things. Why have I said any of these things, come to think of it?"

Chessie shrugged as she got to her feet. "It's me. I seem to have this *power* over people. They look at me and the next thing I know, I'm learning their life stories. But the thing is, I *love* it. Maybe bridal consultants are the female version of bartenders? Now, before you go, let me call my cousin Will."

Elizabeth got to her feet, gathering up the used tissues and shoving them deep in her pockets. "Your cousin?"

"Yes, Will. William J. Hollingswood, Esquire, to be formal about the thing. He's coaching a youth baseball team this summer, which is probably why I thought about T-ball earlier. Let me see if he has room for two more on the roster. If that's okay?"

"It is, but we're not Allentown residents, if that means anything. Richard's house is in Saucon Valley."

Chessie was already dialing a number on her phone. "Nifty neighborhood. But it doesn't matter. Will's is a sort of special team, just created last week. The twins will be fine. Oh, darn, it went straight to voicemail." She put down the phone. "Tell you what, Elizabeth. You give me your number and I'll call you once I've got ahold of Will."

Elizabeth took one of Richard's cards from her purse and turned it over, writing her cell-phone number on the back. "I've only got a cell, but you can try Richard's number if I don't answer. And I can't thank you enough,

Chessie. I wouldn't have had the faintest idea about how to sign the boys up for anything like this."

"No problem," Chessie said, turning over the card. "Richard Halstead, novelist. Nope, don't recognize the name. But don't ever tell him I said that."

"I won't. He writes more for men, I guess. Although he certainly has his share of female fans. Oh, and Chessie? Since Richard will be out of town all next week, and the housekeeper never minds watching the boys, would you…that is, I'd love for you to be my guest for dinner one night."

"Only if we go dutch treat," Chessie said. "And we'll take Eve along, and maybe Marylou—God, we have to take Marylou if she isn't busy with one of her projects. A real girls' night out. I'm guessing you don't have many of those."

"No, I don't," Elizabeth said as the two of them descended the stairs to the first floor once more. "Thank you, Chessie. I'm really, really glad you kidnapped me."

Once Elizabeth had gone, Chessie pulled her cell phone from her pocket and punched in numbers as she headed for her office, away from Eve's always listening ears.

"Will? Yeah, yeah, sorry for hanging up on you a couple of minutes ago, but I just had an idea when I heard your voice, an idea that I think is even better than my original idea, which wasn't all that bad in its own altruistic way, by the way. Although this one could almost be altruistic if you didn't look at it too hard, and—no, I have *not* been drinking. You know I don't drink. Just listen, okay?"

Her cousin's answer was short and to the point.

"Okay, so court convenes again in two minutes and we all know the legal world can't go on without you, except that it's going to, once your suspension kicks in. I'll talk fast, you listen faster. I've got twins, boys, seven years old. They need a youth baseball team."

She pulled the phone from her ear for a few moments while Will gave his opinion of youth baseball teams.

"Right, gotcha. A sin and a shame and a totally over-the-top reaction to your, I'm sure, perfectly calm and reasonable arguments to the judge. No, you're never snarky, especially in court." She laughed. "Yes, now *I'm* being snarky. But my heart goes out to you, it really does. Will you take them? Good. First practice tomorrow morning at nine, got it. Yeah, I know the field. They'll be there. Now, for the second idea. Their mother is a widow, and she needs some fun."

This time she rolled her eyes as she held the phone away from her ear for a few more moments.

"No, she does not bark. No, she does not have a tail. Although the same can't be said for the last blind date you threw at me, buddy boy, so cut that out. You owe me one. You even said so, and I'm collecting, all right? And she's gorgeous, Will, she really is, but maybe a little sad, a little confused."

Chessie sighed as Will tried yet again to hang up on her. "Yes, yes, court awaits. No, I don't want you to be held in contempt again. And no, she's *not* a head case. I said confused, not certifiable. That would be the guy you set me up with at your secretary's wedding reception, remember? Look, I'm not asking you to marry the woman, sport. I just want you to pay her a little attention, that's all. Maybe take her to dinner a couple of times.

"Why? Because she doesn't believe in romance anymore, that's why. I think she's afraid of it, I don't think she thinks she deserves it and I think she's going to make a big mistake if someone doesn't remind her that her hormones are just resting, not gone. Can you do that? Pay her some attention? Nothing heavy, just flirt a little?"

She heard the bell over the front door of the shop ring to announce another customer. Still holding on to the phone, she began making her way to the reception area as Will pressed her to be more specific in her instructions.

"You want *me* to tell *you* how to be charming? Just for God's sake, don't take her to bed. I only want you to wake her up a little, you handsome bastard, you," she ended, suddenly realizing there might be a problem if her plan worked too well. "I mean it, Will. Shake her up a bit so she remembers she's not just a mom, but that she's still young and desirable, and then back off, the way you always do. Nicely! And then we're even, honest. Well, as long as you don't try to throw any more blind dates my way. Agreed?"

She smiled at his answer. "Oh, you egotistical pig—I knew I could count on you."

Chapter Two

Elizabeth pulled her small SUV into a parking space between a battered family van and a shiny black Mercedes-Benz and cut the engine. They were here. At the ball grounds…ball fields…something like that. And twenty minutes late, thanks to a wrong turn off the highway.

"I think that's your team down there," she said, pointing straight ahead at the windshield. "Ready?"

The silence from the backseat was deafening.

"I said," she repeated, unsnapping her seat belt and turning around, "are you ready?"

Mikey took one hand off the handheld game he was playing and held it up, his index finger extended. "Soon as I beat this level, Mom, okay?"

"You'll never beat that level. You always end up zapped," his brother said. "You die like a dog, every time."

Elizabeth reached back and grabbed the game. "Die? Who said you could play games where people die?"

"Oh, Mom," Mikey whined as the game made a sound much like a dying whistle, followed by a splat. "Now you did it. And nobody dies, doofus, so why did you say that? The game is rated E, for everyone, just like it says on the box."

Elizabeth looked at the screen and saw an exasperated-looking duck walking out of a pond on large webbed feet, shaking its feathers and glaring at her accusingly. "I'm sorry, Mikey," she said, handing the game back to him. "Um…better duck next time?"

"Good one, Mom," Danny told her. "Can we go home now?"

It had been a fight all morning. First to get them both up, then to get them to throw on shorts and tops and tie their sneakers—after they'd found their sneakers. Danny's left one had been in the freezer and, no, she didn't ask who had done that, because she already knew. They couldn't decide what they wanted to eat, they needed to brush their teeth—as if either of them ever did that without first being threatened.

Elizabeth got out of the car and opened the rear side door, motioning to the boys to hurry up. "Today, people. Anyone would think you two don't want to play baseball."

"We don't," Danny said, grinning at her, his smile

minus his top two front teeth. "But Richard said we should humor you."

"Oh, he did, did he? Do either of you know what that means? That you should *humor* me?"

Mikey at last undid his seat belt and slid down off the safety booster seat, Elizabeth holding on to his arm as he jumped to the ground. "Not me. I only know that Richard said it's easier to humor women than it is to fight them. Unless you wanted us to eat spinach or something."

Elizabeth's annoyance melted like spring snow under the warm, gap-toothed smiles of her sons. Boys could get away with murder, just with their smiles. Including *boys* who were well into their forties. It was simply impossible to stay angry with any of them.

She made shooing motions with her hands, aiming both boys toward the grassy incline that led down to the small ball field...ball court...whatever.

As she followed them, Elizabeth quickly realized she had already made at least two mistakes, and the boys weren't even officially signed up yet. One, they were the only children wearing shorts, and two, they were the only children not carrying gloves. No, mitts. She remembered that word from Jamie. They were called baseball *mitts*.

Danny and Mikey stopped a good distance from the other children and turned to look at her, their identical big blue eyes that were so much like their father's gazing at her in mute appeal.

"Okay, okay, I'm coming," she said, stepping between them and taking their hands. "Let's look for Mr. Hollingswood, all right? Chessie told him we'd be here."

She walked closer, careful to stay to the left of the long white chalk line that seemed to mark the beginning of the playing area, heading toward a low wooden bench and three men who were watching as the children threw balls at each other. Elizabeth would have thought that they were playing catch, except it didn't seem that anyone was actually catching anything. There was just a lot of throwing and then chasing after the ball going on, except for the trio of boys who were huddled together, examining a worm one of them was holding.

Chessie had said her cousin was a hunk; that was how she'd described him. Elizabeth thought that wouldn't be much of a help until she got closer to the three men. Then it got very easy to pick him out.

He was taller than the other two men wearing matching bright blue T-shirts with the word *Eagles* stitched on the back at shoulder level. He had none of the softness around the gut the others had. He was wearing classy tan Bermuda shorts as opposed to their baggy jeans, and he had his baseball cap on backward, the coal-black hair beneath it looking mussed in the way only great hair can.

Besides, as he raised the reflective, wraparound sunglasses he was wearing, giving her a glimpse of a pair of emerald-green eyes, and started walking toward her, he said, "Elizabeth Carstairs? Hi, I'm Will Hollingswood, Chessie's cousin. These your boys?"

That pretty much cinched it.

"Yes, I'm Elizabeth. And," she said, raising one hand first, and then the other, "this is Danny, and this is Mikey. Boys, say hello to Mr. Hollingswood."

"Coach," Will corrected quickly. "It's shorter. Hi, boys. You like baseball?"

"No," Mikey said, and Elizabeth gave his hand a warning squeeze, so that her son quickly added, "Thank you?"

"Close, Mikey, but not quite the answer I was hoping for," Elizabeth said quietly. "Tell Coach you want to learn how to play baseball."

"But I don't," Mikey, always honest, told her not quite as quietly.

"But we need the fresh air," Danny piped up, always helpful. "And Mom needs the break. That's what Richard says."

Elizabeth looked at Will, who had now pushed his sunglasses up on his head as he gazed at her, his smile wide and white and pretty much something out of a toothpaste ad, if *GQ* even allowed toothpaste ads.

"They really don't know much about sports. I'm sorry."

"Well, this should be fun," he said, and Elizabeth felt hot color running into her cheeks. "Do they have mitts?"

"Uh—no, they don't. But we'll get them in time for the next practice. Is there anything else they need?"

Danny was giving Will his full attention—sucking up, Elizabeth knew was the term for it—but Mikey had pulled an action figure from his shorts pocket and was busily turning it into a truck or something. Neither boy was paying the least bit of attention to what was going on beyond that white chalk line.

"We've got a list here somewhere," Will told her, heading over to a large three-ring binder on the bench. "Did Chessie tell you to bring their birth certificates along and proof of health insurance?"

Elizabeth pulled the relevant papers from her purse. "Yes, I've got all of that right here. Oh, and a check for seventy dollars. Is that right?"

Will took everything from her, looking up at her as he scanned the check but then quickly sliding it into a pocket of the binder without comment. Richard had written the check, and his name was printed on it. She'd argued with him that it wasn't necessary, but he'd insisted. Not that she was going to tell Chessie's cousin that…or that she suspected Richard would have just as happily written a check for two months of sleepaway camp for both boys. He liked the twins. He just didn't have the knack for interacting with them, that's all. He'd rather buy them something; it was how Richard showed affection.

She watched as Will assembled a few papers and handed them back to her along with the birth certificates and her insurance card. "We're a new team, what they call an in-house team, so we only play five other teams. Practices go on just about every morning at nine until our first game, which is also at nine. All the games are played on this field. The schedule and the rules are all on those papers. Six outs a side, no sliding, no stealing, no taking leads and no keeping score so we don't bruise their little egos."

He leaned down to be on eye-level with the twins. "And I don't like this any more than you two do, so let's just try to get through it together with the least amount of trauma, all right?"

He put out both hands, palms up, and the boys surprised her by grinning as they completed the low fives.

"Okay, Danny? Danny, right? Which one of you two peas in a pod is Danny?"

Danny raised his hand. "Me. I'm the good twin. I got all Excellents in Deported."

"Deport*ment,*" Elizabeth correctly quietly, rubbing Danny's blond curls. She really should get the boys haircuts, but she loved their curls. Besides, they had so many years to be grown-up. "And try not to be so modest."

"Huh?"

"Never mind," Elizabeth said, sighing. She'd worried that Mikey would develop a complex about his own C-pluses in *deported,* but since Mikey seemed very happy in his game-oriented world, she had decided not to overreact. "Should they go out on the field now?"

Will shook his head. "No, not without gloves. Not that I think they'll catch anything, but at least they could use them to put in front of their faces if someone puts a little too much on the ball. In fact, today was really just sign-up day, and I think Danny and Mikey were the last two to arrive. We were just about ready to call them all in."

"Oh." Elizabeth nodded, thinking, *Well, that was quick.* And rather a shame, considering how long it had taken her just to get the boys to the field in the first place. "I guess then I'll take them to buy gloves?"

"Rightie or leftie?" Will asked, and she had a feeling those green eyes were laughing at her.

"I beg your—oh. Rightie. Both boys. So I get them gloves that fit on their right hands, correct?"

"On their left hands. Catch with their left, throw with their right," Will corrected. "What kind of glove are you planning to buy? Catcher's mitt? Fielder's glove? First baseman's glove? And they might want their own bats, although we have some here, along with a catcher's mask and pads. Oh, and cleats, of course. They probably should have cleats."

She looked at him intensely, pretending not to see how absolutely perfectly good-looking he was. "And I'll bet you think you're speaking English, too, don't you?"

Will lifted his hat slightly and scratched at his temple as he looked back at the two other coaches before motioning for Elizabeth to stay where she was because he'd be right back.

He walked over to the coaches, handed one of them the three-ring binder, shook hands with both men and then returned to where she and the twins were waiting. "Okay, that's settled. Mitch and Greg have volunteered to finish up here. Let's get these boys some equipment, all right? We can take my car."

"Oh, but that isn't necessary," Elizabeth said, almost

forced to run to keep up with Will's long strides as he headed up the hill toward the parking lot, just as if her *yes* was assumed. "I'm sure I can ask someone at the sporting goods store to help us."

Will turned to face her, although he didn't halt his progress toward the parking lot, walking backward as he addressed the boys. "Who's up for pizza after we get you guys ready to play?"

"Me!" Mikey shouted, punching one arm in the air as he danced in a circle. "Me, me, me!"

"Can I have pepperoni?" Danny asked, not yet ready to commit.

Will looked at Elizabeth. "If your mom says it's all right."

"Mom?"

"This is where I realize I'm beaten and give up and go along, right?" Elizabeth asked, sighing. "Yes, all right. Did Chessie put you up to this?" she asked him quietly as they reached the parking lot. Will was heading toward the black Mercedes, which didn't surprise her. "Helping me with the boys, I mean."

"Chessie? No, she didn't ask me to help you with the boys. Well," he added, his devastating smile back in evidence, "not exactly in those words. Let's take my car."

Elizabeth shook her head. "Can't. Until the boys grow another two inches, they have to ride in safety booster seats. We can follow you, though. I'm parked right here."

Will looked at the small SUV, which was probably

a toy in most men's eyes, then to his Mercedes, and then back to the SUV. "I don't want to lose you in traffic. How about I ride with you?"

Elizabeth did a quick mental inventory of the interior of the SUV, pretty sure there weren't any crumpled fast-food bags or errant French fries on the floor—at least not in the front seat. "Sure," she said brightly, too brightly. "Chessie assured me you're trustworthy."

"No she didn't. Chessie may shade the truth from time to time, but she doesn't outright lie," Will said, leaning closer to Elizabeth so that the boys didn't hear him. "She told me you're gorgeous, by the way. And she's right."

Elizabeth backed up two steps, sure her eyes had gone wide and stupid. "You're…you're flirting with me?"

"Do you mind? Honesty seems to run in our family."

She felt her head moving from side to side. Did this man, this absolutely drop-dead handsome man, just agree that he was flirting with her? Her, Elizabeth Carstairs, better known as *Mom?* Her? "Uh…no?"

They exchanged smiles, Elizabeth rather lost in the moment—someplace she hadn't been in too many years to recall.

Clunk.

"Mom!"

Elizabeth watched as Will's eyebrows shot up even as his head turned toward his car—his beautiful, black, shiny Mercedes.

"Mikey, what did you do?" she asked, already knowing the answer before she saw the SUV's rear passenger door, its edge open against the side of the luxury car. "No! Don't move! Don't touch that door," she said as she raced around the front of the SUV.

"It slipped out of my hand, Mom," Mikey wailed before turning on Danny. "Why didn't you catch it?"

"Coach said we don't know how to catch, remember?" Danny shot back, and then quickly scooted into the backseat and his booster on the far side of the car. Mikey followed him, moving on a par with the speed of light.

"Hands up," Elizabeth ordered automatically, waiting until Mikey had raised his hands above his head so that she knew she wouldn't pinch his fingers when she shut the door. Okay, slammed the door. Then she turned, reluctantly, to see that Will was running his fingers down the side of his own back side door. "How bad is it?"

"I think we're good," he said, wetting his finger and rubbing the tip against the paint. "Yup, we're good. Which is a good thing, because otherwise I was going to have to kill the kid."

"You'd have to get in line to do that. I warn them and warn them about letting go of car doors…"

"Hey, Elizabeth, relax," Will soothed, putting his hands on her bare upper arms. "I was kidding. It's all right. I'm not upset. Accidents happen."

Elizabeth tried to swallow. Her skin seemed on fire where Will's hands were touching her, yet the rest of her body seemed to have gone icy-cold. What was wrong with her? "You…you must have children of your own. To be so understanding, I mean."

He shook his head. "Nope, not even a dog. And no wife, either, since you asked."

She stepped away from his unnerving touch. "I didn't ask."

"Not in so many words, no. But I know you're a widow, so it seems only fair that you should know my marital status. Which is and always has been single." He held up his left hand, fingers spread. "See? No tan line around the fourth finger, left hand. And now that we've got that all out of the way, are you ready to go buy some baseball equipment for these two?"

Actually, she was ready to crawl into a hole and then yank it in after her, but since he probably already knew that, she just nodded as she pulled her keys from her shorts pocket. He snagged them deftly and walked her around the car to the passenger side, opening the door for her.

She got inside. She watched him as he closed the door. She put on her seat belt. She faced front. She folded her trembling hands in her lap. Did her best to remember to breathe.

And, for the first time in too many years to remember, she let events just happen.

It was like shooting fish in a barrel, Will thought, although he'd never held a gun, and the only fish he'd ever seen arrived on his dinner plate, sprinkled with fresh parsley.

Elizabeth Carstairs was one beautiful woman. One beautiful, vulnerable woman. She had a bit of frightened doe about her, yet she was certainly take charge when it came to her sons, who seemed to know she had limits and carefully avoided them.

Will was pretty sure he could have Elizabeth in his bed without much effort and without even breaking a sweat. Except he was also pretty sure that was not what Chessie wanted him to do. All right, so he knew it wasn't what Chessie wanted him to do. In fact, she'd probably hunt him down and strangle him if he took the flirtation business that far.

No, he was here to wake up the slumbering Widow Carstairs, make her feel desirable and female and—didn't the woman own a mirror? Damn, she was gorgeous. Skin like honey, soft brown eyes that betrayed her every mood. She would be wise to never play poker.

Then there was that fantastic jawline that the style of her streaky blond curls turned into a regal work of art. A tall, slim body, with curves in all the right places. And those long, straight legs. A man could easily fantasize about those legs.

What the hell was the matter with Chessie? She knew he wasn't a saint. She sure as hell had to know he wasn't a damn martyr. What did she think she was doing, throwing a woman like Elizabeth Carstairs into his lap?

And one more thing. Why had he wanted to punch Greg in the chops when he'd winked and made a fairly obscene pumping gesture when Will had told him he was taking Elizabeth and her sons to lunch? Greg hadn't meant anything by it, at least nothing men didn't think about and say to each other all the time.

It just didn't seem right to make jokes about a woman like this one.

Will looked over at her as he stopped for a red light on MacArthur Road. She'd been quiet for the last ten minutes as they'd been pretty much stop-and-go in mall traffic. "You all right?"

"Excuse me? Oh. Oh, yes, I'm fine. You're really being very nice." She turned to look at him with those soulful brown eyes. "I mean, you aren't married, you have no children of your own. And yet you're coaching a baseball team."

"Chessie didn't tell you?"

"Tell me what?"

The light turned green, and Will pulled out quickly, knowing he had to get over into the right lane in order to pull into the next mall in a line of malls and other stores that took up a good two miles on both sides of MacArthur Road. "She didn't tell you that I'm a lawyer. Defense lawyer. One with a big mouth sometimes. And, thanks to Judge Harriette 'The Hammer' Barker, who has a fairly perverted sense of humor, it was either she slapped me in the local lockup for repeated contempt of court, or I volunteered to take over as head coach for a new baseball team that needed one. Her grandson's on the team, you understand. And thinking of that leaves me wondering what she's got against her grandson."

"So...so you didn't want to coach the team?"

"Not even in my dreams. But I may be changing my mind."

"Because you like teaching seven-year-old boys to play the game?"

"No, I don't think I'd go that far. But I do like big brown eyes."

Elizabeth opened her mouth to say something, maybe something like "Get out of my car, you pig," unless, if he was lucky, he hadn't pushed too far, too fast. But, thanks to the twin terrors in the backseat, Will was pretty sure he'd never know.

"You said I could have a turn. Come on, gimme!"

"I'm not done yet. I've still got one more life left. Hey! Let go of my arm, doofus, I have to get to the safety zone before—"

Whirrrrrrrrr...splat.

"Mom!"

Still with her gaze on Will, Elizabeth put her arm between the seats, reaching into the backseat. "Give. Now."

"But Danny did it, Mom. It's my game."

"And now it's mine. *Give.*"

A small red plastic game and equally small set of headphones were swiftly deposited in the glove box, and the boys in the backseat were silent for several seconds until Will heard a whispered, "See what you did? It's all your fault."

"Shoulda shared, Mikey," Danny whispered back.

Elizabeth made a small sound in her throat, rather

the way someone might attempt to gently shush someone who was speaking in a movie theater, and the backseat was silent once more.

"How many children are on this team of yours?" she asked him, just as if the interruption had never happened.

The question seemed to come out of left field. "Sixteen. Thirteen boys, three girls. Why?"

"Oh, nothing. Except you might want to reconsider the local lockup offer. Cracking rocks or making license plates would probably look like a walk in the park after dealing with sixteen young darlings like my two back there. And don't tell me you haven't noticed."

Will pulled into a parking space near the door of the sporting goods store. "You know, you may have a point. Do you think I might have a case against The Hammer for cruel and unusual punishment?"

"I'm not a lawyer, and so far you've only had one day on the job, so that remains to be seen, doesn't it? Seven-year-olds aren't really that terrible, if you know how to handle them."

"Oh, and how do I do that?" Will asked once they were out of the car, and Elizabeth had a firm grip on one hand of each of her twins.

"Be fair, be consistent, choose your battles," Elizabeth told him as they crossed the driving lane and reached the sidewalk outside the store. She let go of the boys' hands and they raced for the door, arms waving, each wanting to be the one who caused the sensor to activate the automatic doors. "And two things more.

Never underestimate the inventiveness of a seven-year-old…and never let them see you sweat."

"They can smell fear?" Will asked, one eye on the twins, who had come to an abrupt halt just inside the doors, as if they'd never been inside a sporting goods store before. Which they probably hadn't. Poor kids.

"I'd rather say they can sense weakness. It's one thing to try to be their friend, but there's a line between adult and child, and you cross it at your peril. Unless you want to be treated like you were just another seven-year-old boy."

"Not if their mom is going to take all my goodies away, no," Will said, and watched as becoming color ran into Elizabeth's cheeks. Yup, shooting fish in a barrel. Taking candy from a baby. And she'd think it was all her idea. "Come on," he added, taking her hand as if it was something he did all the time, "I think the baseball equipment is over there, to the left. Boys? Follow us."

Two hours, about two hundred fifty dollars and two pizzas later they were back at the ball fields and Will was handing Elizabeth the keys to her SUV as she joined him outside the drivers' side of the car.

"Sticker shock wear off yet?" he asked her.

"You know they're going to grow out of those baseball shoes before the season is over, don't you? At least you said the hats and shirts come as part of the registration fee," she said, smiling weakly. "But they seem more excited about the idea of playing now, don't they?"

"I can think of something that might make them even more excited. I've got four box seat season tickets for the Pigs, and they're playing at home tonight."

"The Pigs? I beg your pardon? Don't pigs have something to do with football?"

"That's pigskin, another name for a football. I'm talking about the IronPigs, our local Phillies baseball farm team. We could take the boys."

Elizabeth shifted those marvelous eyes left and right, as if searching for understanding. "Why would anyone want to be called Pigs?"

"The name wouldn't have been my first choice, either, but it's catching on."

"All right, if you say so. But what's an iron pig?"

Will thought about this for a moment. "Well. Iron pigs are what they poured steel into? Or maybe it's a twist on pig iron? I know the name has something to do with the local Bethlehem Steel Works plant, back when steel was the largest industry around here, instead of the casino that's operating on part of the old plant grounds now."

"In other words, Counselor, you don't know what an iron pig is?"

"I haven't got a clue," Will answered truthfully. "Does it matter?"

"To you or me? Maybe not. But do you remember being a seven-year-old boy, Will?"

Will considered this for all of five seconds. "I'll find out. But I'm betting I'm not going to be able to discover why the mascot is a huge fuzzy brown pig named

FeRROUS, and they'll probably ask me that, too, right?"

"If they don't, I know I will."

"Thanks for the warning and, I hope, for accepting my invitation. The game starts at seven, and there's always a lot of entertainment for the kids between innings. What do you say?"

"I…um…" She looked into the backseat, where the twins were using their new mitts in a sort of duel with each other. "I suppose so. They really don't seem to have a single idea of what baseball is all about, do they?"

"It doesn't look like it, no," Will told her in all honesty. "But that's not your fault."

"Because I'm a woman," Elizabeth said, "or because I don't have a husband to teach them?"

Will mentally kicked himself. "I'm sorry, Elizabeth. That didn't come out the way I meant it. Not that I'm sure I know what I meant. I don't have kids, but if I did, and they were girls? I'm pretty sure I wouldn't be up on all the…girl stuff."

"So baseball is boys' stuff? Didn't you say there are three little girls on the team?"

Will sighed. "You're doing this on purpose, right? And I'm moving too fast. Do you want me to take back my invitation?"

She bit her bottom lip as she shook her head in the negative, those entrancing thick ribbons of blunt-cut curls moving with her and making his palms itch to run through her hair. "I haven't been on a date since…but this isn't a date because Danny and Mikey are going with us, so…so I don't know why I'm being so obnoxious. We'd love to go see the IronPigs with you."

"Great," Will said, belatedly realizing that he really cared about the answer Elizabeth gave him. Him, the guy who saw women as pretty much interchangeable— and always replaceable. But he wouldn't think about that right now. "Let me get the boys their shirts and caps from the back of my car. They can wear them tonight."

Chapter Three

Elizabeth left the twins with Elsie, Richard's house-keeper, in the kitchen, where they were proudly showing her all their purchases, except for the bat their mother had insisted remain outside a house filled with antiques and lamps and other treasures that probably should not come in contact with a seven-year-old and his new toy.

She ducked into the powder room just off the kitchen to wash her hands, splash cold water on her face and make use of the toothbrush she kept there, as she felt fairly certain she had pepperoni breath.

Then she went in search of Richard, who was most likely in his study, killing somebody.

She knocked on the door and poked her head into the

large, cherrywood-paneled room that overlooked the swimming pool, the tennis court and a seemingly limitless expanse of well-designed grounds. "Richard? We're back."

Her employer, friend and possible fiancé looked up at her blankly for a moment before his busy brain hit on the "Oh, it's Elizabeth" switch, and then returned his attention to the computer monitor in front of him. "Home from the baseball wars, are you? That's nice, Elizabeth. Tell me, what's another word for *incomprehensible?* As in, she experienced an incomprehensible reaction."

"Inconceivable? Unfathomable?" She thought about Will Hollingswood—why, she didn't know. "Inexplicable?"

"Yes, that last one. Definitely containing more of a hint of sexually motivated confusion. That's perfect," Richard said, his fingers flying over the keys for a moment before he sat back, smiled at her. "I'd use the thesaurus that comes with this *incomprehensible* new computer program, but you're faster and less likely to have me crashing the machine."

"You'll get used to it," Elizabeth said, walking over to the huge U-shaped desk that had been custom-built for Richard, and subsiding into the chair she sat in when he wanted to watch her face as she read his work. "You had to change programs to be compatible with the new operating system."

"True enough. But in my next book I think I'll devise an untimely and considerably messy end for some software mogul. Remind me, all right?"

"Wasn't it enough that you dropped that cheating tax collector off a conveyor belt and into a vat of hot latex meant for condoms?"

"Ah, yes, the Triple-Ripple Extra Sensitive Deluxes, weren't they? Only barely enough, Elizabeth. Nothing is too undignifying a death for a tax collector." He pushed his computer glasses up high on his head, where he would soon forget they were, just as Chessie had said.

"I don't think *undignifying* is really a word, Richard."

"No? It should be," he said, rubbing at his jaw, shadowed a bit in a mix of brown and gray day-old beard. "Didn't shave this morning, did I? Well, I'll do that before dinner, I promise. I've, well, I've been on a roll today. So, tell me. How did the boys enjoy their first day of baseball?"

As she told him about the field, and the boys throwing balls and then chasing them because nobody seemed able to catch them, and recounted their shopping trip and pizza lunch—leaving out mention of Will Hollingswood for reasons she wasn't about to examine at the moment—Elizabeth looked at Richard, telling herself yet again that he was a very handsome man. A very nice, gentle, sweet and caring man.

His sandy hair was always too long and a bit shaggy, but she couldn't imagine him any other way. He may be getting just a little thicker around his waist, but he was still a very fit man. He played golf twice a week and had his own fully equipped exercise room he used…well, when he remembered to use it.

His eyes were brown, like hers, but rather deeper-set, the lines around them a sign of too many hours in front of the computer but flattering in the way that wrinkles made a man more interesting while they only made a woman look older.

Yes, he was a handsome man. If he was, again, a woman, he'd be described as a well-preserved forty-five. As a man, it would more probably be said that he was just entering his prime. And she was twenty-eight, not exactly a teenager. That wasn't so terrible, was it?

Chessie had seemed to think so. Or were her reservations centered more on what she saw as other problems?

"Richard?" she asked when he didn't smile as she finished telling him about Mikey's horrified reaction to learn that there would be *yucky girls* on his baseball team. Girls and seven-year-old boys were like oil and water, it seemed. "Have you been listening to me?"

"Yes, of course. The boys bought mitts and gloves and shoes. And bats! Let me reimburse you for those. God knows you're grossly underpaid. Your employer should be shot."

His eyes kept drifting toward the monitor. Elizabeth stood up and walked around the desk, placing a kiss on his cheek. "You will not pay for their equipment, thank you. You've already paid for their registration. And now I'll leave you alone because obviously I've interrupted you at some crucial moment in your story. But, first, may I see?"

"I don't think it's quite ready for prime time, Elizabeth," he said, moving the mouse to one of the corners of the monitor, so that the screen went black. "I'm trying something new, you understand."

"But…but you're in the middle of a book."

"That can't be helped. Sometimes a writer has to take a voyage of discovery, follow his muse where it leads. Or at least that sounds important, doesn't it? Truthfully, I'm pretty much stuck on how to work the next scene in the current manuscript, so I'm playing with an idea I had the other day."

"A new character?"

"No," he said, looking somewhat sheepish. "A new genre. James Patterson does it. Others have done it, are doing it. Why shouldn't I? I'm writing…trying to write…a love story."

Elizabeth was dumbfounded. "A love story? You mean a romance?"

"No, my dear. When women write such books, they write romances. When *men* write them, they're love stories."

"What's the difference?"

"Respect. Men get points for sensitivity and women get slammed for being sentimental and encouraging their readers to believe in fairy tales. Equality may be written about in books, but the publishing industry, or at least the critics and reviewers, are pretty much the last to acknowledge the fact."

"And that bothers you?"

"Enough that John and I are going round and round about this book, if I do write it, if he can place it,"

Richard said, referring to his agent. "What do you think of the pen name Anna Richards? My mother's maiden name."

Elizabeth shook her head. "You really plan to publish this book as a woman? Why?"

Richard pushed his chair away from the desk and stood up. "Why, so I can have it announced two weeks after publication that I, Richard Halstead, darling of the critics, am the real author."

"Because you don't think the reviews will be as good as they are for your other books," Elizabeth said, nodding. "But, Richard, what if they are?"

"Damn. I hadn't thought of that one." He pulled her toward him and gave her a kiss on the forehead before slipping his arm around her waist and guiding her toward the doorway. She could have been his daughter, or his collie, Sam The Dog. "See why I need you, Elizabeth? Now I'm going to have to rethink the entire thing, aren't I? Oh, and I have some news."

"Really? I've only been out of the house for a few hours, and already you're writing a roman—a *love story* and changing your name while you're at it."

"Not anymore. I think I'll stick to my own name. I'm sure John will thank you for that. And I'm not even sure I'll finish the book. I've only just begun it, and I'm honest enough to tell you that it isn't as easy as I thought it would be. Killing people is much less complicated than dealing with all these emotions. But, no, my real news is that I'm leaving tonight for my tour, heading to New York to do the *Broward* show."

"Richard!" Elizabeth hugged him in genuine joy. "I know how you've longed to do that show. What a coup."

"There was a cancellation so I'm a second choice but not too proud to grab at it. But now I have to ask you to pack for me. Only enough for two days, and you can forward the rest of my luggage on to Detroit, my original launch city. Do you mind?"

"Mind? Of course not. It's why you so grossly underpay me, remember?" she said with a smile, beating down a selfish and probably dishonorable little voice inside her that was saying, *Now you don't have to tell him about Will. Not that there's anything to tell him. Really.*

"I should have you writing my dialogue for me," he said as he paused at the door, clearly escorting her out of his sanctum so he could get back to his love story, but doing it in such a tactful way that she really couldn't mind. "John's arranged for a car to pick me up at four, and he and I will have supper at my hotel. I'd hoped we could dine together tonight, Elizabeth, perhaps talk a bit more about…my proposal."

"That would have been very nice. But we wouldn't want to be rushed about things, would we?" Elizabeth said, clutching at straws.

Richard frowned as he looked down into her face. "I should take you to Rome. Or Paris. Be more romantic."

Elizabeth raised her hand to his cheek. "You have a deadline. You have this book tour. I understand."

"I'll always have a deadline, Elizabeth," he reminded her. "I'll always have half my head living in a world filled with my own creations. There's a part of me that's still a selfish child, playing inside my own imagination. I'm not offering you a lot, am I?"

"You've offered me everything you can give, and I'm more grateful than I can express. If…if I could just have a little more time…"

"Yes," he said, his eyes lighting up. "That's precisely what she needs to say to him, and in just that way." He gave Elizabeth a quick hug. "What would I do without you?"

"I have no idea," Elizabeth said quietly as she watched Richard hurry back to his computer. How strange. This morning, she would have been flattered and taken his words as yet another reason she should accept his proposal. But now? Now she felt no real satisfaction in being Richard's assistant, Richard's muse, Richard's very good and comfortable companion. And she hated herself for that lack.

And then she tilted her head to one side, watching him as he attacked the keyboard. Why was Richard suddenly writing a love story? A week ago, before his proposal, he'd been deep in his book, racing through the pages as if there weren't enough hours in the day to get all of his ideas down.

So why this switch? Was he feeling the same lack she was? Was he still, in his own way, searching for something more? Something that, for all their compatibility and friendship, he knew he hadn't found in her?

And if she hadn't met Will Hollingswood this morning, would she even be asking herself any of these questions?

Elizabeth checked on the twins, was assured by Elsie that they were fine with her, helping her mix up a batch of peanut butter cookies, and then she went upstairs to pack Richard's suitcase.

"Oh, my," Elizabeth said as they walked into the ballpark and the field opened up in front of them. "I had no idea there was anything like this in the area. Boys, look over there," she said, pointing to the large scoreboard above center field. "There's the IronPig."

They'd entered the ballpark through gates that led to a wide concrete area wrapping around the field above the main seating area that stretched from where they were, right field, to behind home plate, and then stretched out again along the left field line. It was as if they were standing on the rim of a bowl, with the rows of seats ahead of them leading down to the natural grass field itself.

Will stepped up behind them, looking across the outfield at the huge pink snarling pig head that made no sense, yet somehow seemed to make perfect sense…if you didn't mind wearing shirts and hats with steroid-strong cartoon pigs on them.

"Pig iron, boys," he said, "is a sort of in-between product that's a result of smelting iron ore with coke and…some other things. It's used to make steel, like for bridges and buildings. At one time, the Bethlehem Steel Works plants in, well, in Bethlehem, which is right next door to Allentown, made some of the best steel in the world. Bethlehem steel was used, for instance, for the Empire State Building and the Golden Gate Bridge in San Francisco, and even in the reconstruction of the White House. You know, where our president lives."

Danny, or maybe it was Mikey, turned his head to look up at Will as if he had been speaking Greek. "Uh-huh. Can I have some cotton candy? Some of the blue kind?"

"What? Oh, sure, no problem," Will said, leading them all toward the kiosk displaying bags of pink and blue cotton candy. "I thought you said they'd ask," he said quietly to Elizabeth. "I've got the whole story, mostly. Although I didn't think I'd mention the part where the molten iron was poured into a long channel and then these forms sort of branched off all along the sides of the channel, and somebody decided the whole thing looked like a litter of piglets, you know, feeding from the mother sow. Pigs, iron—pig iron."

"You were probably wiser not to get that involved," Elizabeth said, clearly trying to hold back a smile but not succeeding. "You really looked up the definition of pig iron, and all that information about the steel plants? That was very sweet of you."

He pulled out a ten-dollar bill to pay for two bags of cotton candy and got four ones back in change. At least somebody was operating on a pretty hefty profit margin these days. "But not entirely helpful. I couldn't find anything about how pig iron got turned around into iron pig, and I still sure as hell don't know why anyone would name a baseball team the IronPigs."

"Well, I'm beginning to think it's rather cute. And you have to admit he's a pretty ferocious-looking pig. Oh, look, they have a store. Is there time for me to take a look around before the game starts?"

"If you let me stay out here and wait for you, sure," he told her, already eyeing the line in front of the beer stand. "Would you like me to get you something to drink?"

"Thank you, yes. I'll have a lemonade if they have any. And apple juice or something for the boys? It might help wash some of that sugar off their teeth."

"You've got it," he told her, looking at the boys, who were both already sticky with cotton candy, their fingers, cheeks and definitely their tongues turning a deep shade of blue. "Uh, I shouldn't have let them have that, should I?"

"Cotton candy wouldn't have been my first choice, no. But they both ate all of their supper, so it's all right. At least they're not asking to go home. But you know what? I don't think I should take them into the store while they're all sticky like that, do you? Could you watch them for me? I want to get them each something with the pig on it."

Panic, swift and fairly terrible, kicked Will in the midsection. He suddenly remembered why he'd always made it a point to never date women with children. "Me? Watch them? Oh," he said, attempting to look, if not fatherly, then at least reasonably competent. "Sure, no problem."

"Thank you," she said, rummaging in her purse.

"Here's some wet wipes in case they finish their cotton candy." Elizabeth's smile strangely made his sacrifice seem worth the effort, and he held out his hand as he mutely accepted the wrapped packets. He then watched her disappear into the crowd milling along the walkway behind the right field seats, feeling only slightly desperate.

"Okay, boys, let's go get Coach a nice cold one."

"A cold what? Can we have one, too? Where's Mom?" one of them asked, the one who had somehow gotten cotton candy on his elbow. *How the hell did you get cotton candy on an elbow?*

"You've got to be Mikey, right?"

"Yeah. So where's my mom?"

"She went to buy you guys some Pigs stuff. She'll be right back." *So please don't cry.*

"Cool," Mikey said, licking his fingers. "I'm thirsty. Hey, Danny, are you thirsty?"

Danny, who had wandered off without Will realizing he was gone, walked back to them wiping his hands together after tossing the empty plastic bag in a garbage can. At least they were…*trained.* "Sure. I saw a kid with a hot dog. We could get hot dogs. Or maybe pizza? I saw some pizza, too."

Will was beginning to sense that Elizabeth's sons were going to eat their way through their first experience at a baseball game.

"Here, hold out your hands," he told them, ripping open one of the packets. With memories of his mother scrubbing at his sticky face and hands with a washcloth, he started by wiping their faces and then opened two more packets and gave them each a wet towelette so they could clean their own hands. He reserved the last packet for himself, to clean himself up after cleaning them up.

"Will? Will Hollingswood? Is there something I should know?"

Will shut his eyes for a moment, recognizing the voice, knowing who would be standing behind him when he turned around.

"Hi, Kay," he said grabbing the used towelettes the twins were shoving at him and stuffing them in his pocket before turning to look at the tall, stunningly beautiful brunette. "I didn't know you liked the Pigs."

"Well, then that makes us even. I didn't know you had children."

"Very funny. They're not mine, Kay."

"Are you sure?"

"Okay, not so funny this time. Kay, look, I'm sorry I didn't call you, but it's been a hell—" he shot a quick look at the twins, who weren't really paying attention, thank God "—a heck of a week."

"Yes, I heard about The Hammer. Are these two of your little baseball team children?"

"They've never seen a baseball game," Will answered, going into lawyer mode. Tell the truth while saying nothing.

"And the entire team is here somewhere? You're really taking this punishment seriously, aren't you? Or maybe just trying to score brownie points with The

Hammer, which wouldn't be a bad idea. You really were out of line, Will, you know."

"So says the assistant district attorney. If you'd been sitting at the defense table, you would have objected, too."

Kay shrugged her bare shoulders. She was dressed in a sort of tube top that didn't quite reach her waist, and a miniscule tan skirt whose length only barely passed the public decency test. It was like there were two Kays, the buttoned-down prosecutor in the courtroom and the sensual, sexual shark everywhere else. He should know.

And he needed her gone before Elizabeth got back.

Besides, the twins were now running in circles in a small cleared spot near the beer stand, chasing each other and nearly bumping into people, including a guy built like a Mack truck and carrying a full tray of beers. He didn't look like the kind of guy who'd just laugh and say "boys will be boys" if the tray hit the ground.

"I've got to go, Kay," he told her, pointing to the twins.

But he'd left it too late, because here came Elizabeth toward him, carrying a large plastic bag with the image of an IronPig on it.

"Danny! Mikey! Get over here."

The twins stopped running and raced to their mother, each of them grabbing for the bag. She pulled out a pink baseball hat with the IronPigs logo on it and then handed the bag to her sons. "You each have the same thing, so there's no reason to kill yourselves trying to see."

Then she looked at Will. And saw Kay.

"I'm sorry I took so long, Will. There was a line at the register. Hello," she said to Kay.

Will didn't physically step between the two women, but he did think about it. "Elizabeth Carstairs—Assistant District Attorney Kay Quinlan."

"Oh, how formal, Will," Kay said, extending her hand. "Outside the courtroom, I'm just Kay. Are these two adorable boys your sons?"

"Only mostly adorable, but yes, they're mine."

Will grabbed the twins and stood them in front of him, his hands on their shoulders. Not that he needed a shield from either woman. "Mikey, Danny, meet Assist—that is, meet Ms. Quinlan."

The boys mumbled something that sounded vaguely like a greeting and then went back to their new possessions, matching baseball caps and a pair of tan canvas-covered stuffed dogs sporting blue bandannas with the IronPigs logo on them.

Elizabeth must have seen him looking at the dogs. "They're autograph hounds. I thought if I could interest the boys in the players that they'd also become more interested in the game. The salesgirl told me the players often sign autographs before and after the games. Is that all right? Oh," she added, reaching into her purse, "I also got them a set of trading cards with the players' photographs on them. Although the roster—roster, right?—isn't complete anymore because players are always coming and going. Some of them have gone up to the big show already this year."

"The big show?" Will grinned at Elizabeth's earnest expression. "You mean, the big leagues, up with the Phillies."

"If you say so. She just said the big show. I'm sorry, Kay. This is all new to me—and to the boys. Will has been kind enough to help explain the game to them now that they're on a team."

"So they are on your team?" Kay asked, one perfect eyebrow arched. "The one that only came into existence in the last few days? My, my, William, you don't let any grass grow, do you?"

"Excuse me," Elizabeth said, taking Mikey's hand, probably knowing that where one twin went the other followed. "I think Mikey would like a hot dog. We'll be right over there, Will. Kay? So nice meeting you."

Will waited until Elizabeth and the boys were standing at the back of the line at the hot dog stand and then turned back to glare at Kay. "You had to do that?"

"Probably not. She seems like a nice woman. Let me guess. Newly divorced?"

"Widowed."

"Even worse. Shame on you. Well, at least now she's been warned, hasn't she? When are you going to make your move, Slick?"

"I'm not making a move, Kay."

"Sure you are. And the sooner you make it, the sooner you'll be back in the pool. Call me."

"I'm not making any— Oh, the hell with it," he said as Kay turned away, heading for the beer kiosk.

He stood where he was for a few moments, his thirst

for a beer gone, and wondered how he was going to explain Kay to Elizabeth. *She's nobody important, just someone I sleep with once in a while when we're both bored?* No, that wasn't going to cut it. Did he have to say anything at all? Probably not, at least not from the way Elizabeth had looked at him before taking the boys to the hot dog stand.

How the hell had he gotten into this mess? Okay, so he knew how he'd gotten into the mess. He should never have tried to set Chessie up with somebody, especially with anal-retentive estate lawyer Bob Irving. Payback was a bitch, but what was fair was fair. And the idea had seemed simple enough. Show the girl a good time, Chessie said. Flirt with her, make her feel feminine, desirable. Remind her she's still young—and all that crap.

Sure. Great plan.

Then have her standing there all fresh-cheeked and vulnerable, with her mommy-clothes yellow blouse and knee-length denim skirt and her silly pink IronPigs baseball cap on, and two cute but definitely not disposable kids with her, and introduce her to the sleek, sensual, übersophisticated, smart-mouthed Kay Quinlan.

That ought to help Elizabeth come out of her shell, or wherever the hell place it was that Chessie seemed to think she needed to get out of. *Not.*

Then again, who needed this? Not him. He didn't like kids, didn't know how to relate to them. Cleaning off sticky faces definitely wasn't a turn-on. Nor was trying to romance a woman whose kids kept getting in the way.

He looked over at the hot dog stand to see that the boys were now munching happily as Elizabeth squeezed mustard on her own napkin-wrapped hot dog. They were kind of cute kids, though. Maybe they needed a haircut. All those curls on boys old enough to be swinging a baseball bat? He'd be surprised if they weren't teased in school. But a woman raising her boys alone maybe wouldn't know the little ins and outs of boy stuff. The kids could have a problem.

"Nah. Mikey would sock anyone who teased him," Will told himself quietly. "And Danny would talk the rest of them to death."

Will frowned. How did he know that? He'd only been with the twins for a couple of hours that morning. But he was already beginning to be able to tell them apart just by their mannerisms, the way they talked, the words each of them used. The way Danny played his mother like a fine Stradivarius, the way Mikey couldn't seem to stand still for more than five seconds at a time.

The blare of the loudspeaker on a nearby pole alerted Will that the team was taking the field, snapping him out of thoughts that weren't making him all that happy anyway.

He walked over to Elizabeth and told her it was time to take their seats. They filed into the box in the third row behind the dugout just as it was time to stand for the national anthem. Elizabeth yanked Danny's baseball cap off just as Will was doing the same for

Mikey—their nearly synchronized movements seeming so natural to him and maybe even satisfying. Elizabeth smiled at him in thanks for his help, and he suddenly had a niggling feeling that, although he was the only one who hadn't had anything to eat yet tonight, he'd maybe just bitten off more than he could chew.

"I still can't believe they sell turkey legs at a ballpark," Elizabeth said as Will eased his car into the line of traffic leaving the ballpark. She felt so comfortable with him now that it was difficult to believe she'd been nervous and vacillating up until the moment he'd picked them up for the game.

"I still can't believe Mikey *ate* one," he told her, waving his arm out the window to thank the trucker who'd let him in line. "Plus the slice of pizza and the snow cone."

"And the hot pretzel—although, to be fair, you ate at least half of it," Elizabeth told him, taking off her baseball cap and running her hand through her curls. "And we won. You do realize that now the boys will expect fireworks if their team wins a game."

"We don't keep score, remember?"

"…four…five…hey, Mom, I've got six autographs," Danny called out from the backseat. "And Mikey got seven. But we can get more next time, right?"

"Yeah, Mom. Next time. When are we going again? I love the Pigs. Oink! Oink!"

Elizabeth and Will exchanged looks. "Methinks you've created a pair of monsters, Coach. I don't know how much they understand now about baseball, but they certainly understand all that food and getting autographs."

They were free of the parking lot now, and Will deliberately turned left as most of the traffic was turning right. The trip home might be longer this way, he told Elizabeth, but at least they wouldn't be sitting in traffic for the next quarter hour.

"No problem. I told you, I have season tickets. But I'm afraid the team leaves for a road trip tomorrow morning. A road trip, guys, means that they'll be playing their games in somebody else's ballpark. They won't be back here for another week or even longer."

There were twin sighs of frustration from the backseat that were not matched by the occupants of the front seat.

"They'll be fine," Elizabeth assured him. "With luck, they'll also both be asleep by the time we get back to the highway. We all really did have a wonderful time tonight, Will. Thank you."

"Actually, thank you. That was a lot of fun, explaining the game to the boys. They asked some pretty good questions, too."

"But I didn't?"

He shot her a grin. "Oh, I don't know. The one about why the players don't wear dark pants so that they don't get so dirty wasn't too terrible."

"They were wearing *white*, Will. Who plays in the dirt while wearing white? I pity whoever has to presoak all those uniforms."

"But they're the home team, Elizabeth. The home team wears white. It's…tradition."

"And it's a tradition that would only last another three days if the team owners had to personally presoak the uniforms themselves," she said firmly. "Don't say anything. I know I'm being silly. I just couldn't think of anything else to ask you. But I think I cheered at the right times." She turned slightly in her seat and looked behind her. "Ah, out cold, the pair of them. And we didn't even reach the highway yet."

Worse, Elizabeth thought, with the twins asleep, and the subject of the baseball game pretty much worn out, now she had to find something to say to Will to keep the conversation going. She dredged her mind for a topic, being very careful to avoid the subject of the beautiful and clearly well-known-to-Will Kay.

Not that his relationship with the assistant district attorney had anything to do with her. Because she and Will weren't on a date. You don't take a pair of bottomless pit rowdy seven-year-olds with you on a date. Not a *real* date….

Chapter Four

Will had turned on the radio, and they'd allowed the music to fill the silence for most of the ride back to Saucon Valley.

He'd asked Elizabeth if she'd seen Billy Joel's Broadway musical, *Movin' Out,* the one that featured the singer's hit song, "Allentown."

She hadn't, but she did know the song. That led to a short biography, as she thought of it, and Elizabeth told him how she'd grown up in Harrisburg, the state capital, but she and Jamie had moved to the Allentown area to follow a job transfer.

"When he died, my mother wanted me to move back home, but I was young and stupidly independent. I knew if I moved home, my mother would turn me back into her kid again, take charge of my life. I was a mother now, and I had to learn to stand on my own two feet, raise my boys. At least that's what I thought. Stupid, huh? With them barely out of diapers, I certainly could have used the help. But my mother's gone now—she moved to Sarasota, that is—and I've learned to feel like this area is our home."

"And now you're working for a famous author, Chessie told me."

"Richard, yes." She looked out the window as they drove past the large three-story mansion—there was nothing else to call it but a mansion. "You came in through the gates earlier, but if you drive past them, there's another lane you can use to get straight to the guesthouse and garages."

"Okay, I see it," Will said, and in another few moments they were in sight of the large stone-walled bank of garages. There was a light burning at the top of the outside staircase and the small landing that was there and another in the kitchen lit up two of the windows. "How old is this place? Do you know?"

"Richard says the main house was built in 1816, but the garages were added much later, along with several additions to the house itself. It's difficult to tell, though, as the stone is such a good match. The original Halstead homestead was part of a very large farm."

Will pulled his car to a halt behind Elizabeth's and put the transmission in Park. "Halstead." And then he said it again. "Halstead...oh, now I remember. There's an old oil painting of a Judge Halstead in the courthouse. Very imposing man. I have a feeling a lawyer who spoke out of turn in his courthouse probably ended up in the public stocks. Or maybe his wig just itched."

"He wore a wig?" Elizabeth eyed the staircase to her apartment. She wanted to be up there, safely on the other side of the door. What was the matter with her? She hadn't been nervous earlier. Why was she nervous now? "That must have been a long time ago. Well... well, thank you again, Will. The boys and I really had a nice time."

Will shifted on his seat, looking over his shoulder. "You're going to need help with these guys. They're out cold. And I'd love a cup of coffee, if you don't mind."

He'd love a cup of coffee. Of course he would. It would only be polite to ask him, too. Elizabeth Carstairs, you're hopeless!

"Oh, yes, of course," she said, opening her door before he could come around and do the courteous thing. The date-like thing. "You'll have to pop the child locks," she reminded him.

She then opened one of the back doors while he opened the other and, together, they looked at the sleeping twins. Danny had used his autograph hound as a sort of headrest, and Mikey—oh, oh, *Mikey*—had his thumb in his mouth. He only did that when he was exhausted. Her heart melted.

"Come on, boys. We're home. You have to get up now," she told them, reaching in to touch them each on the cheek. So soft, so warm. Her babies. "Mikey, come on, sweetheart. Danny?"

"I'm thinking a megaphone," Will said, grinning at her across the expanse of the backseat. "Or maybe dynamite."

Elizabeth shook Mikey's bare leg and then unhooked his seat belt. "Mikey. Michael Joseph Carstairs. Wake up!"

"Wake up, it's time for bed. That makes sense. That's a mother thing, isn't it, passed down from generation to generation," Will said, unhooking Danny's seat belt. "Look, Elizabeth, I have an idea. You run ahead and open the door, and I'll carry them upstairs, one at a time."

The idea made sense. Perfect sense. Well, perfect sense to someone who hadn't been both mother and father to the twins since they were three. She was used to handling the boys on her own. She was independent. She was capable. She was being an idiot….

She reached into her purse for her keys. "I can manage Mikey," she said, already pulling the boy's pliable form toward her. "Fireman's lift. It works." She took Mikey's new hat from him, stuck it on her own head— what else was there to do with it?—hefted her son over her shoulder and then retrieved the autograph hound, tucking it under her other arm. Her knees wanted to buckle slightly, but she ignored their protest. "Ready?"

"As I'll ever be," Will told her, putting Danny's new IronPigs hat on his own head before grabbing up Danny and his autograph hound. He then kicked his side door shut, so that Elizabeth did the same thing, and, together, they made their way up the flight of wooden stairs to the landing.

Fitting the key in the lock wasn't easy, but she managed, even while mentally trying to remember if she'd moved the laundry basket from the kitchen table, where she'd earlier sat sorting socks and little boy underwear. One look inside the kitchen told her that she hadn't. *Some people use fresh flowers as a centerpiece,* she told herself as she led the way through the apartment, flipping on lights as she went.

"Right through here," she said as they passed by her bedroom and she turned into the larger of the two bedrooms, the one shared by the twins. Bending her knees, she managed to pull back the covers and then gratefully lowered Mikey onto the mattress. "If he'd had one more hot dog tonight, I wouldn't have been able to manage this," she said, watching as Will untied Danny's sneakers and pulled them off.

Did Will know he was still wearing Danny's hat? The hat didn't quite fit, and he had it on sideways. Did he know how adorable he looked?

"Sorry, I think the left lace is still knotted," he said, now tackling Danny's socks. "Nothing seems to be waking them, does it? I don't remember the last time I slept this well—or this deeply."

"The sleep of the innocent," Elizabeth told him, pulling the covers up over Mikey's chest. They could take baths in the morning. A little dirt wouldn't kill them, nor would having them sleep in their clothes.

"The innocent, huh?" Will said, smiling at her as they walked out of the darkened room. "That explains it. I haven't been innocent in a long time."

She shot him a weak smile as she leaned past him to close the bedroom door. "You've still got Danny's hat on, you know."

He reached up and took it off, handing it to her before reaching for Mikey's hat, which was still on her head. "Long live the Pigs."

"Oink, oink," Elizabeth said, putting the hats down on the hall table. "This way they'll be able to find them first thing in the morning. I have a feeling I'll be seeing a lot of that pink pig."

"I'm trying to figure out how you manage two kids at one time. I mean, I can see how you do it now—and you do it very well. But what about when they were younger? One is a handful. Two is twice that."

"I had my ways," Elizabeth told him as they passed back down the hall, her bedroom to their left, a combined living and dining area to their right. "When I needed to carry both of them, I'd pick up Danny first and then let Mikey climb me."

They entered the brightly lit kitchen, and Elizabeth headed for the automatic coffeemaker she'd already prepared for the morning and switched it on.

"Excuse me?"

She turned to rest her hip against the counter. "I'd hold Danny, and then Mikey would grab on to my hand with both of his and put his feet against my leg. I'd pull, and he'd *climb*. Once he was high enough, he'd sort of snuggle against me and I could hold him." Elizabeth felt her cheeks growing hot. "Sort of like King Kong climbing the Empire State Building."

"Except that you're a lot more soft and *snuggly* than good old Bethlehem steel," Will said, looking at her in a way that made Elizabeth think perhaps what little makeup she wore had smudged beneath her eyes or something.

"I...I have some cookies in that jar on the table. Peanut butter. The boys made them today with Elsie, Richard's housekeeper. They're very good."

"That sounds nice, yes," Will said, stepping closer to her, which wasn't a huge feat, as the kitchen wasn't all that large. "Here," he said, reaching toward her, "let me fix this. Your button must have come open when you were carrying Mikey."

Elizabeth looked down in shock to see Will's tanned hands, his long fingers, working with the material of her blouse that had, indeed, come open, revealing the line of her fairly utilitarian bra. He didn't linger, didn't do anything more than slip the button back into its button-hole, but Elizabeth had to fight a shiver at the unexpected intimacy.

He looked into her eyes. He smiled. His eyes smiled. Teased. Then he backed off.

"Coffee's ready," she said, turning to grab two mugs from the cabinet, congratulating herself for not having fainted dead away or begun drooling or some such idiocy. "What would you like with it? Sugar? Cream?" *Me?*

"I'm fine with it black," Will told her. "Where should I put this?"

She looked over her shoulder to see he was now holding the laundry basket. Was any of her underwear in it, or just all those little pairs of briefs with cartoon animals or superheroes or race cars all over them? "Oh, anywhere," she said lamely. "That shouldn't have been there. I'm sorry. I don't have guests very often."

Will pulled the cookie jar to the center of the table and removed the lid, reaching inside to grab one of the cookies. "Don't worry about it. You have two kids, and you have a full-time job. I may have a full-time job, but the rest of my life is my own. Do you have your own life, Elizabeth?"

The suddenness, the seriousness of the question, startled Elizabeth. "I'm very happy," she answered, wondering if she sounded as defensive as she felt. She also realized that she hadn't answered Will's question.

So, obviously, did he. His eyes, his slight smile, both hinted to her that he did. But his next question really proved it.

"When was the last time you went out for dinner, Elizabeth? Not counting taking the boys someplace where you order by talking into a clown's mouth or a dinner that could be served on a napkin at a ballpark?"

She couldn't remember. Dear God, she couldn't remember! "I don't know. A while?"

"Okay. How about this one. Name the last movie you saw in a theater."

Elizabeth wanted to get up, leave the room. Will was a lawyer, and he was interrogating her. But why? "It was…something the boys wanted to see. There was this prehistoric cartoon squirrel, and he was always chasing a—I don't *know*. What difference does it make?"

"None, probably," Will said, sitting back in his chair,

the coffee mug—the one with a superhero dog stamped on the sides—clasped in both of his hands. "You'd never been to a baseball game until tonight. That was setting the bar pretty high. I didn't want our next date to be a letdown. So dinner and a movie?"

She carefully set down her coffee mug, which was better than having the hot liquid splash all over her fingers because her hand was shaking. "Tonight was a date?"

"Technically, probably not. I thought we could try again, this time without the kids. Not that I don't like them," he added quickly. Too quickly?

"No, of course not. You were very good with them. Very…understanding. But I—I don't date. I mean, I haven't been on a date since before I was married, and I really don't know how to—" She looked at him in appeal. "Could you help me out here? I'm being an idiot."

"Happy to be of service. A date, Ms. Carstairs, consists of two people who wish to—"

"I know that part, smarty-pants," she said, and then winced. Who called a grown man *smarty-pants?* Women whose usual verbal confrontations begin with "take your fingers out of your mouth, young man, and answer me," that's who. "How about I just say yes? I would love to go to dinner and a movie with you."

"Terrific." Will stood up at the same time she did, which brought them into rather close proximity to one another. "Tomorrow night?"

"I'll need to arrange for a babysitter," she said, not backing up because that would be so *obvious*. "I think Elsie wouldn't mind. Thank you."

"No, thank you," he said, looking at her with those marvelous eyes of his. "Do you like Italian?"

She nodded. "I love Italian, yes."

He opened his mouth, hesitated. "Good. Italian it is."

There was a tension between them Elizabeth knew someone could cut with the proverbial knife.

"Italian it is," she repeated, taking a deep breath.

"You can pick the movie. As long as it isn't a court-room drama. I always want to start shouting at the screen when they get it wrong. I might embarrass you, not to mention getting us both thrown out."

"Thanks for the warning. I'll look for a comedy."

"Good idea." He stepped closer to her. "I'll pick you up at six. We'll eat first and then go to the late show."

"Sounds…sounds like a plan."

Would he just *do* something? Talk, not talk. Move, not move. Kiss her, not kiss her. Something!

"I had a very good time tonight, Elizabeth," he told her.

"And that surprises you?"

He ran a hand through his hair, mussing it in a most appealing way. "You figured that out?"

She nodded. "I just haven't figured out why you invited us."

His eyes shifted slightly, but then he looked at her as if he didn't have a secret in the world. "You haven't looked in a mirror lately?"

"Oh." *Well, there's an answer that will go down in history!* "I…I wasn't fishing for compliments. But…but thank you."

"You're welcome," Will said, and then he moved

even closer, and Elizabeth knew what was coming next. He was going to kiss her. She'd been out of the dating game for a lot of years, but she recognized a move when one was being put on her.

She lifted her face so that she could meet him halfway. If nothing else, curiosity was winning out.

"Mom? *Mom!* Can I get out of bed? I'm thirsty!"

Will stepped back. "I thought it would take fireworks to wake up those kids."

"Or the sound of a pin dropping on cotton. They have an inner sense that tells them when I've just slipped into a bubble bath or I just picked up the phone to call my mother—that sort of thing. I don't know how they do it, but they do it. I'm sorry, Will."

"I should be going anyway," he told her, heading for the door. "Practice is at nine tomorrow morning."

"Mom!"

"Yes, I'll…we'll see you then. And we did have a wonderful time tonight."

She closed the door behind him, fought the urge to lean herself up against the wood and sigh a girlish sigh and then headed for the cabinet to get Mikey a glass of water. No, she should make that two glasses of water, or Danny would be sure to ask for one. And then, with them both awake, they really needed to brush their teeth and get into their pajamas and…

She nearly dropped the glass when she heard the knock on the door.

"It's only me, Elizabeth," she heard Will call through the door.

"Uh…it's open?"

He stepped inside, holding on to the pair of child booster seats. "I figured you might need these," he said, putting them down on the table.

"Oh, yes, of course. I'm sorry I didn't think of that. Thank you."

"You're welcome. Oh, and one other thing."

Elizabeth gripped the glass tightly. *Here it comes. He's going to kiss me. What do I do if he kisses me? Close my mouth? Open my mouth? Fall on the floor in a dead faint?*

Will walked past her to lift the lid on the cookie jar. "I thought I'd take one for the road," he said, holding up a cookie like some sort of prize. "See you tomorrow."

"Yes…see you tomorrow," she echoed, lifting her hand to give him a small finger-wave.

This time, after the door closed, she counted to ten, waiting to hear his car move off down the drive.

Then she sat down in one of the kitchen chairs and laughed until Mikey padded into the room to remind her he was still thirsty.

Once back on the main road, Will used his hands-free cell phone to call his cousin. She answered after five rings, her voice sounding as if he'd woken her up. *Good.*

"Chessie, this isn't going to work."

"Wha…who—Will? What time is it?"

He shot a look at the dashboard clock. "Not quite

midnight. And I mean it, Chessie. This isn't going to work. I'm going to call it off."

"You're going to call what off? For God's sake, Will, it's midnight. Just because you can operate on less than eight hours' sleep doesn't mean the rest of us can. Call me back in the morn— Oh, wait. Um…does this have anything to do with Elizabeth? I thought you told me you were just taking the three of them to a ball game. Ah, man, Will, what did you do?"

"Nothing," he told her, looking to his left before pulling out onto the highway. "I did nothing, I should do nothing, I am doing nothing. It was a stupid idea, Chessie. She's not my type."

"If you mean she isn't cold and ambitious and only out for herself, then no, she isn't."

"Leave Kay out of this," Will told her, concentrating more on his driving than he was on what Chessie was saying. Always a mistake.

"Aha! So you knew just who I meant, didn't you?"

"Never mind that. I'm just telling you—"

"Never mind that? You wake me up in the middle of the night, and then don't even give me a moment to gloat when I score a major hit? Hi, Will, this is Chessie—remember me? I *gloat*. I live to gloat."

"Yeah, yeah, score one for Chessie. Can we get back to the reason I called, please? Because your plan is full of holes, Chess. There's no such thing as just waking someone up. You have to figure out what to do with them once they're awake."

"You could be nice and hang up and call them again

in the morning," his cousin said. She then added quickly, "Okay, okay, I know you're not talking about me. You're talking about Elizabeth. What did you do, Will? Turn on all your boyish charm in one go?"

"This has nothing to do with me. I'm only saying that Elizabeth...that she's..." How about that? Him, the silver-tongued lawyer, at a loss for words. "She could get hurt."

He could hear Chessie getting out of bed. Well, either she'd thrown back the covers and gotten out of bed, or she had just levitated a good three feet above the mattress. "William Hollingswood...what...did...you... do?"

"*Nothing.* I didn't do a single thing. All right, almost. I was going to kiss her good-night. Hell, it's the natural end to an evening. But I didn't. Chessie, I don't think the woman's been out on a date since her husband died. How do I say this and not have you crawl through the phone and murder me? Okay, I can't. She's *ripe,* Chess. Ripe for the plucking."

"But you won't...pluck. Right?"

Will closed his eyes for a moment. "No, I won't. But she knew I wanted to. She's a nice woman, Chess. A lady, a mom, for crying out loud."

"Not your type."

"God, no."

"Did you *want* to kiss her? Or was this one of those, 'oh, hell, we're here, why not' deals?"

"I don't know," Will said honestly. "What I do know is that Elizabeth is the forever type, and I'm not. On my own I never would have asked her out. So, since you're the one who got me into this, how do I shut this thing down without hurting her?"

His cousin was silent for a few moments, and then surprised him. "There's a *thing?* Really? You know, Will, it could just be that Elizabeth doesn't find you all that captivating. Did you think about that one? Okay, so you took her out. One time. Do you really think you've now ruined her for all other men or something? God, that's arrogant."

"You're right." Will pulled into his own driveway and cut the engine. "It was one date. And not even a date, since we had the twins with us. It was just a friendly evening. I'm overreacting," he said, sitting back in the bucket seat. "Of course I am. I'm being an ass, and I'm sorry. And I've already asked her out for tomorrow night. Why did I do that, Chessie?"

"Yes, you were, and I have no idea. Unless, of course, Elizabeth packs more of a punch than she thinks she does. Does she, Will? Is this phone call about you being worried about her or you being worried about yourself?"

"Go back to bed, Chess," Will said, cutting the connection. And then he sat in his car for another five minutes, trying to answer his cousin's question. "One more day. I'll give it one more day," he said at the end of those five minutes, and then he went inside, feeling he'd at least begun to back away...even if Elizabeth didn't know that yet.

Chapter Five

Sam The Dog had somehow managed to wrap his leash around Elizabeth's bare legs in the time it took to grab a folding lawn chair from the back of the SUV, and the boys were already halfway down the hill to the field by the time she could follow them.

She felt a small pang as she watched them so blithely desert her—and not only because they'd left their bats and mitts behind in the backseat. They were growing up. Sometimes it was as if they grew an inch or more overnight, and they didn't seem to need her the way they once had…the way she'd always clung to them, probably too tightly, once Jamie was gone.

They'd just finished first grade, had been away from her for nearly seven hours a day. Now they were playing baseball. Tomorrow they'd be leaving for college.

"And now let's all have a pity party for the overprotective mommy in the crowd," Elizabeth grumbled as she struggled to hold on to chair, bats, gloves and Sam The Dog while navigating the slope down to the ball field. "Sam The Dog! Stop pulling on the leash!"

Her mother would have told her that she was attempting a "Lazy Man's Load," trying to carry too much at one time in order to save herself a trip back up the slope to her car, and that the exercise was doomed to end in failure. And her mother would, as usual, have been right.

The lawn chair slipped out from beneath her arm, cracking her hard on her ankle bone before it hit the grass. Her reaction was to reach down to grab her ankle, a move that dislodged the two bats tucked into the crook of her other arm. She made a quick, twisting grab for them, and that's when it happened.

Sensing the slack on his leash, Sam The Dog made a break for it, heading straight onto the field and into the midst of the players standing huddled around the coaches.

It was like watching a bowling ball strike the pins, sending them scattering everywhere.

Sam The Dog, being a border collie, immediately began trying to herd all the children back to where they were, even while the coaches seemed to be attempting to shoo him off the field.

Elizabeth left everything where it had fallen and

took off down the slope. "Sam The Dog! Sam The Dog, you come here this instant! Danny, grab his leash!"

Danny made a valiant stab at it but only ended up laid-out on his belly as Sam The Dog eluded him as he circled the children, urging them closer and closer to the pitcher's mound.

She saw Will standing near the players' bench, a clipboard against his chest, watching the excitement with an amused smile on his face. She hastened to where he stood, nearly breathless from running and shouting. Well, at least now she didn't have to worry anymore about what she was going to say to him the next time she saw him.

"I'm so, *so* sorry," she told him as Mikey finally managed to grab Sam The Dog's leash. "He means well. He really does."

"Mikey or the mutt?" Will asked her, his eyes still on the ball field. "He was herding them, wasn't he? And with much more success than we've been having. Amazing. If we can find him a shirt that fits, we could make him the first-base coach. What's his name? I heard you calling something, but I couldn't catch it."

"He's Sam The Dog," Elizabeth said, relieved that she and the dog weren't going to be immediately ejected from the field.

Will turned his attention to her. "You're kidding, right? And you call him that? Not Sam? Sam The Dog?"

"He's Richard's dog. Officially, he's Samuel Thibold Devonshire, I think it is, but Richard thought that was too long, so now he's Sam The Dog. I don't know. It fits somehow."

"True, I guess. But it's so obvious. I mean, if you called him Sam The Deer that wouldn't be so obvious. Sam The Donkey? Sam The Duck? Or, to make it simple, you could just call him STD."

At this, Elizabeth narrowed her eyes as she looked at him. "STD? I don't think so."

Will smiled, covering his mouth with his hand. "Oh, right. That would seriously cut down his chances with the lady dogs, wouldn't it?" He took two steps toward the field. "Mikey! No dogs on the field. Bring him over here."

There were protests from the team, all of whom seemed to be almost as enthralled with Sam The Dog as he was with them.

"Come on, put some hustle into it. We've only got the field for another hour or so."

Elizabeth took the leash from Mikey, telling him to get Danny and run back up the hill to get their equipment and her chair. "Once again, Will, I'm really sorry. But Richard is gone, and Sam The Dog looked so forlorn as I was leaving that I thought it wouldn't hurt to bring him along."

"Richard's gone? Richard as in your boss—that Richard?" Will asked, as if that was the only thing he'd heard. "For how long?"

"We're not sure. His publishing house keeps wanting to add new cities to his tour. A week, ten days—more? Why?"

"No reason," Will said, taking Sam The Dog's leash from her. "I think the pooch here will enjoy himself more if I tie him up next to the team bench. And I just thought that might mean you're pretty much on vacation, with your boss gone."

Elizabeth mentally, figuratively—please, Lord, not physically, because that he could see—backed up a pace. "I have a few things to do, routine things. But yes, I suppose you could say I'm on vacation."

"Then you'll be staying here in town, not going anywhere. Not taking the kids to the shore or anything?"

She shook her head. "No, I hadn't planned on it. Why?"

He seemed to mentally pull himself up short. "No reason. It's just that we need to field ten kids—we have four outfielders, cuts down on the coaches having to chase balls—and we only have fifteen on the team. I'll be down two for a week when Jason and Drew Keglovitz leave on vacation. So…so it's good to know that Mikey and Danny will be available. Sam The Dog, huh?"

Elizabeth nodded. "Sam The Dog. Right. Well, um, I should go find a place that's out of the way and let you get back to work."

"Okay, good. I'll…I'll see you after practice."

She turned away, her eyes momentarily widening in a "what the heck was that all about?" way before she picked up her lawn chair and headed for the grassy area where other parents were congregated.

"Here, put your chair down next to mine," one of the women, a striking redhead, said, motioning for Elizabeth to join her. "Cute dog. I'm Annie Lambert. My

Todd is the one with the bright orange hair—no surprise there, right? Which little darling is yours?"

Elizabeth introduced herself as she unfolded her chair and sat down. "I've got two here, actually. Mikey and Danny. They're twins."

"Oh, how neat. Unless you're the one up all night with them while they're newborns, I guess. I swear, my Todd never slept through the night until he was three— years, not months. Where are they?" Annie asked, shading her eyes with her hand as she looked out over the ball field.

Thanks to her evening at the IronPigs game, Elizabeth was able to answer with some authority: "Danny's standing at first base, and Mikey is at third."

"Really? You have to mean the ones with those adorable blond curls sticking out from under their caps. I'm so sorry. I thought they were girls." Annie pulled a comical face. "I was told there were a couple of girls on the team. Not that I don't love curls, and I would hate to see them cut off. It's bad enough their soft baby skin doesn't stay that way. Todd's got knees like sandpaper. He's also got his hair shaved down to just about nothing for the summer, but that was his father's idea. I think it's great that your husband is letting you keep their curls this long. They grow up too fast as it is."

"I'm a widow," Elizabeth said, as if that excused the curls, which was ridiculous. The curls were probably ridiculous. Why hadn't she realized that? But they were babies, her babies. And now they were growing up so fast. "They need haircuts, don't they?"

Annie put her hand on Elizabeth's arm. "Sweetie, you do what you want to do, and don't listen to anyone else. They're your kids. But, yeah, I'd say get them haircuts. Kids can be cruel."

"They never told me about any problems in school," Elizabeth said quietly. "But you're right. My husband would have made sure the curls were gone by the time they were three or four. It's just so difficult sometimes...letting them— *Ohmigod!*"

As she and Annie had been talking, Elizabeth was also watching the practice on the field. Will was throwing balls high into the air, and the fielders—they were called fielders—were running in to catch them. Trying to catch them. Watching the balls bounce and then chasing them.

It had been Danny's turn, and he'd run in from left field just as the other players had done, opened his mouth wide just as the other players had done and held out his huge glove, just as the other players had done.

Except instead of catching the ball, or wildly swinging at the ball with his glove or watching the ball bounce and then chasing it...Danny had just stood there, and let the ball hit him on the top of his head. He immediately clapped both hands to his head and fell to the dirt, yelling, "Ow-ow-OW!"

"Steady, girl," Annie said, swiftly grabbing Elizabeth's arm as she half rose out of her chair. "The coaches will handle it. The last thing the kid needs is Mommy running out onto the field."

"But he's hurt."

"It's a rubber ball. Sort of. He'll be fine. Besides," Annie said as Elizabeth sat down once more, "he's got all those curls to act as a cushion. There, see, he's up and going back to the base to try again."

"They should have been girls," Elizabeth lamented. "I'd know what to do with girls. But I'm an only child. I don't have a brother—or even any male cousins. I'm flying blind here, Annie. That was okay when they were younger. But now…?"

"Now you follow your instincts."

"Really? My instinct was for me to go running down there onto the field, remember?"

"Right. You figure out what your instincts tell you, and then you do the opposite."

Elizabeth laughed and then pointed to the field. "Look, he caught it this time! *Yea, Danny!*"

Her son heard her and looked up the hill and then smiled and waved.

"Okay, I feel better now. Anything else I should know?"

Annie shook her head. "No, now it's my turn. How well do you know our hunky coach?"

"Will?" Elizabeth didn't know how to answer that. "Uh…I only met him yesterday. Why?"

Annie leaned closer to her and spoke quietly. "Word is he's quite a hit with the ladies, as my mother used to say. Handsome, rich—all that good stuff. But also the love them and leave them type."

"Really," Elizabeth said just as quietly, and a quick vision of Kay Quinlan popped into her mind.

"I'm just saying, you know? He's not here because he loves coaching kids or anything. He's here because otherwise he'd be in the lockup for talking back to some judge. He might be looking around, thinking there has to be a way he can have some fun, as long as he has to be here anyway. You're young, you're pretty, you're available. And I saw the way he was looking at you earlier. I'm not insinuating anything here. Like I said, I'm just saying, you know?"

Elizabeth nodded, looking down the hill to where Will was now showing Mikey how to hold a bat. The man didn't look as if he wished he could be somewhere else. He looked as if he was enjoying himself. He'd looked as if he'd enjoyed himself at the sporting goods store, at the pizza shop and at the ball game last night. But what did she know about how anything *looked?* "Thanks. Not that I think you're right. But I'll keep your warning in mind."

"Hey, don't do it for me. The man is a dreamboat. I'd say go for it."

"You're suggesting a fling, Annie? Is that it?"

"As someone who hasn't *flung* in a long time? Yeah, I suppose I am. I'll just live vicariously through you. And look—no, don't look! But he was just looking up here, and he wasn't looking at me."

Elizabeth kept her head down, pretending to search for something in her purse. She looked, she hoped, calm, cool and completely collected. But inside she was already up and out of her chair—running for her life.

* * *

Elizabeth had already folded up her lawn chair and said goodbye to Annie after the two of them exchanged phone numbers and a promise to take all three boys for lunch after the Saturday-morning game.

Elizabeth knew she could count her friends on one hand, and even those she'd known in the apartment building where she'd lived until moving into Richard's guesthouse had sort of faded away in the past ten months. In truth, her friends had been little more than the mothers of other children the twins played with in the park. Her life had been much too busy and much too lonely once Jamie got sick and after Jamie died.

Living at Richard's estate had cut her off even more, she realized with a bit of a start. Other than phone conversations with his agent, publicists and others, her life had pretty much revolved around Richard; Elsie the housekeeper; Barry, the sixtyish man who took care of the grounds; and the twins.

Well, she was on a first-name basis with two of the checkers at the local supermarket. But that probably didn't count.

So it was nice feeling connected to other women again, however tenuously. First Chessie at the bridal salon and now the bubbly Annie.

She was even developing a social life. Dinner and a movie with Will tonight; a planned dinner with Chessie and her manager, Eve D'Allesandro; and now talk of an outing with Annie and her family. She'd soon have to buy her own electronic day planner, she thought with a small smile.

Elizabeth watched from behind the bench as Will and the other coaches handed out some papers to the team and then reminded them that bats and bases and batting helmets didn't pick themselves up and stuff themselves in the canvas equipment bags on their own.

Mikey, who didn't seem to know there was a hamper in his closet, immediately raised his hand, volunteering to go bring in second base, and went running off to do just that. Danny was already sliding bats into a long canvas bag, without being asked.

"Way to show initiative, Curly," one of the coaches said, rubbing Danny's head as he passed by him.

Danny winced at the nickname, and so did Elizabeth.

Her cell phone began to vibrate in the pocket of her shorts. She put down the folding chair and pulled out her phone, looked at the displayed number, and then lifted the phone to her ear. "Hello, Richard," she said, turning her back on the crowd of children and coaches—and Will—and walking a few feet away. "How was the interview? I taped it, but I had to get the boys to baseball practice, so I didn't see it yet. I didn't want to feel rushed when I— Oh, that's wonderful!"

She listened, making what she hoped were intelligent comments at appropriate times, as Richard told her all about his interview and about the room-service breakfast that didn't arrive, so that he had made a pig of himself in the green room and ended up going onto the set with powdered sugar on his tie.

"Speaking of pigs," she said when Richard was done with his news, "the boys and I went to an IronPigs game last night." She nodded as she turned around, pushing her hair out of her eyes as the breeze kicked up, watching Will lift two heavy canvas gear bags up and onto his shoulders as if they were stuffed with marshmallows. "No, it was fun," she assured Richard, who seemed surprised at her news. "Richard? Do you think the boys need haircuts?"

She frowned at his answer. And then she tried to tell herself he wasn't so uninvolved with the twins that he hadn't really noticed their hair.

"That's very polite of you, Richard, but surely you have an opinion. No…no reason you *should*. I just thought you would, that's all. Well, tell me this, then. Do you think Mario would cut the boys' hair?" She squeezed her eyes shut for a moment. "*How* much? For both of them or just one of them? *Each?* You're kidding! That's…that's just out of the question. *No,* I won't have Mario put it on your tab. Don't be ridiculous. I'll see what I can do. When's your next interview?"

After warning her that he'd be flying to Chicago at seven that night and probably would be out of touch for the evening, Richard hung up—but only after reminding her to stay out of his office and consider herself on vacation until he returned.

She closed the phone, feeling suddenly lost, cut off and extremely uncomfortable at how easy it was that Richard hadn't planned to call her again tonight.

And then, shockingly, following hard on the heels of her momentary unease, Elizabeth realized she also felt good. Very, very good.

Unencumbered. Or at least as unencumbered as the mother of two can ever feel.

And young. She felt young. There had been days, weeks—years—when she'd felt as old as time and just as weary and burdened.

But today? Ah, today the sun was shining. She'd made two new friends. She was on vacation for at least the next week, with nothing to do but be with her boys, to please herself, to remember that she wasn't even thirty yet, let alone as old as time.

And a man had noticed her. Oh, certainly Richard had noticed her...noticed her as much as Richard noticed anything, bless his heart. But when Will looked at her she *felt* noticed. And young. And...yes...desirable.

He made her tingle. She would admit that to herself because there was no sense in pretending she hadn't felt it. That awareness, that sure and certain knowledge that he was man and she was woman. Whether they knew each other well or not, *chemistry* was happening.

Elizabeth put her hands to her suddenly burning cheeks, and that's when she realized she was smiling. *Oh, what a naughty girl you are,* she thought. *How long has it been since you've been naughty?*

"Elizabeth?"

She broke out of her thoughts when she heard Will call her name and saw that he had picked up her lawn chair, the twins standing on either side of him, holding all of their own gear.

"Oh, we're ready to leave? Here, you have those bags. I can carry my own chair."

"That's all right. We'll all heading in the same direction. Dan's okay, by the way. Aren't you, Dan The Man?"

"It was only a ball," Danny grumbled. "But you're still buying me a water ice, right?"

"Danny!"

Will grinned at her. "Bribery," he explained. "When tears threaten, bribery is always an option. Do you mind?"

She looked at her watch. "I suppose a water ice wouldn't ruin their lunch. But don't you have to get to court or something?"

"No. Along with playing baseball coach, I've been barred from stepping foot in the courthouse for two weeks now that I wrapped up my last case on the docket. I only had a couple of pretrial things going on anyway, and they've been pushed back until next month, courtesy of The Hammer. Since I'm my own boss, I've juggled some appointments and decided that every hardworking lawyer needs a vacation now and then."

"That's nice. Richard always says that there are benefits and problems in being self-employed. The benefit is that you're your own boss and can work when you want to, but the downside is that you're your own boss and it doesn't pay to coddle your employee."

"I'd say Richard has a point. I've been known to beat myself up rather badly when I'm facing a trial deadline. I've often thought of reporting myself to authorities for not paying myself some pretty hefty overtime."

They'd reached the parking lot, and Elizabeth hunted in her purse for her car keys, clicking on the button that opened the back hatch of her SUV. Will had done much the same thing with his Mercedes while the twins piled into her backseat and strapped themselves into their booster seats.

"Today I'll just follow you," she told him. "I want to take the boys to the mall after you pay off on your bribe, to see if I can find one of those walk-in hairdressers for them."

Will cocked one well-defined eyebrow at her. "Heard that, did you?"

She shook her head. "Heard what? Oh, you mean how one of the coaches called Danny, Curly?"

"Okay," he said, nodding. "We'll go with that one."

"What? What did I miss?"

"Nothing. When the team was in line to get their handouts one of the boys called Mike, Mary. Mike didn't notice, so I let it go. But I was going to try to figure out a way to tell you it might be time for the twins to lose the curls."

"You were going to do that?"

He held up his hands as if in self-defense. "I know, I know. Butting in where I don't belong. It's just…it's just that you don't have anybody to help steer you through the waters on this stuff, as it were. I noticed, that's all."

Richard didn't. The thought came to Elizabeth's mind, and she guiltily shooed it away, telling herself that Richard was Richard, and it was all right that he didn't notice things. Like the new dress she'd bought last week. Or the fact that she'd cut her hair.

"Elizabeth? Honest to God, I'm not trying to tell you how to raise your sons. God knows it's none of my business. And you'd already decided to get them haircuts, right?"

"Annie—Todd's mother—thought they were girls," Elizabeth told him. "So, yes, I'd already decided. And their hair isn't *that* long, is it?"

"No," Will said quickly. "It's the curls, and the being blond, I suppose. And they're how old now, seven?"

They're my babies. They're all I have. "Yes, all of seven. But I refuse to shave their heads. I don't care what other parents do. I've always trimmed their hair myself. Do you know of a good salon?"

"You don't want a salon, Elizabeth. You want a barber. And, yes, I do. I think Sid gave me my first real haircut a million years ago. Well, over thirty years ago. And you know what, I have an idea."

"Oh, you do, do you?" Elizabeth felt that go-with-the-flow thing sneaking up on her again. "And am I going to like this idea?"

"Maybe not, but I think the boys will. See, I remember my first haircut. I remember the tickle of the electric trimmer on the back of my neck. I remember the oil Sid slicked over my hair. I remember the lollipop he gave me. And I remember my mother sitting on a chair over in the corner, crying because I didn't look like her baby anymore."

Elizabeth bit her bottom lip for a moment. "You're thinking I might cry and make a fool of myself as those beautiful blond curls hit the barbershop floor."

"Might? No, that's probably pretty much a given. I'm thinking Mike and Dan will be embarrassed that their mother is crying. I know I was. So how's this for a plan? I pay off my bribe to Dan, then I drop you at the mall and we plan to meet somewhere in about two hours—after Sid has done his thing."

"Oh, I don't—"

"It's a guy thing, Elizabeth. A man thing."

She closed her eyes for a moment, actually believing she could see Mikey and Danny smiling and waving as they flew away from her, flapping the little wings on their backs, going off into the big bad world without her.

"A man thing. I understand." She looked up at Will's open, smiling face. "And you're laughing at me, aren't you?"

"Only a little. It's just hair, Elizabeth. They aren't running off to join the circus or anything."

"And Sid? Is he good?"

"I still have both my ears, don't I?"

"Oh, I give up," Elizabeth said at last, handing him the keys to her SUV. "I'm just going to go with the flow."

"Sometimes that's the only way to travel," Will said, opening the driver's side door, leaving her to walk around the front of the SUV and help herself into the passenger seat. Which wasn't very romantic of him.

Then she wondered why that bothered her.

They met at the food court three hours later. A very long three hours later, although Elizabeth felt they had been hours well spent. Will had called her cell phone from the parking lot, and she had immediately ordered vegetable pizzas, two lemonades and two iced teas. Her haul was already on the table in front of her, waiting for the others to arrive; her small mound of packages sat at her nervously tapping feet as she tried to sit quietly, pretending she wasn't a nervous wreck.

She'd bought a new dress, a sleeveless cotton sheath that was on sale—half off—which didn't make it any more lovely than it already was. The lower price just seemed to make its hot pink color more reasonable, considering she felt the need to buy accessories to go with it: a small shoulder purse of baby-soft ivory leather, a drop necklace of pink and lime-green stones that matched her new lime-green strappy heels. She'd even visited the cosmetics counter to splurge on new lipstick and blusher to complete the outfit, which really hadn't been complete until she'd also purchased a new plunge bra and some bikini underwear that promised not to show panty lines.

She liked thinking about the new dress, the jewelry, shoes and cosmetics. She'd consider the bra an impulse buy and tried not to think about it at all.

Then she bought each of the boys new talking race

cars they'd asked for when the race cars she'd bought them for Christmas became obsolete thanks to the just released talking versions. Toys, she'd long ago decided, were like cereal and laundry products. The manufacturers were always bringing out new and improved versions to get you to buy them again.

With her stomach rumbling as the aroma of the pizza escaped the closed box, she stood up beside the table she'd chosen, scanning the shoppers for her first sight of her newly shorn sons. When she saw them coming toward her, she sat down again all at once, her knees having lost the ability to keep her upright.

Was it their haircuts? Was it the now darkly blond slicked-down hair so neatly parted on the left, just the way Jamie had worn his before the chemo took it all away, so that they showed their resemblance to their father in a way she had never noticed before this moment? Was it how handsome they both looked, how happy they both looked…how grown up they both looked?

Or was it the easy way they walked hand in hand with Will, chattering up at him, not even bothering to look for her, so happy to be with him. What had Will said? Oh, yes. How could she forget: "It's a man thing."

And it was true, it probably was. And one the twins had no experience with, or at least no memory of, poor things. A male figure in their lives. A father figure in their lives.

"Oh, God…"

Elizabeth got to her feet again as she tried to collect

herself and then called out as brightly as she could, "Hello! Will? Who are those two strangers you've got with you? I bought Danny and Mikey the new cars they wanted—but I don't see them anywhere."

"Mo-om," Danny complained, rolling his eyes. "It's us. Stop kidding."

"It is? Oh, my goodness, it is! Well, don't you two look handsome!"

"The curls are still there," Will told her as the boys scrambled into seats, and Mikey all but ripped off the top of the pizza box. She loved vegetable pizza—the boys never even realized they were getting all that broccoli into their tummies. "Sid just put some kind of taming gel on them for now. I bought the boys some and left it in the car. So, what do you think? You're not going to burst into tears or anything, right? I promised Dan and Mike you wouldn't."

Dan and Mike? He kept calling them Dan and Mike. What happened to Danny and Mikey? Elizabeth felt a sense of panic rising in her. *Please, somebody, stop the world. I want to get off!* Something inside her screamed. "No, I'm not going to cry," she said, not looking at either twin, or at Will, either, for that matter. "I saved some of their curls from the first time I cut their hair. If I get too maudlin, I'll just pull out those bags and hide in my room as I sob like a *girl*."

She dared to take another look at her sons. "They…they really look like their father now."

"Do they? I imagine you'd know. But even though they're supposed to be identical, I think Dan looks a lot like you when he smiles. And there's something about the way Mike uses his eyes that reminds me of you."

Elizabeth reached for a slice of pizza even as she looked toward Will, just to give herself something to do, because her appetite had completely deserted her. "How he uses his eyes?"

"Yes, exactly like that."

"Like what?"

"The way you just looked at me. Your head tipped forward just a little, so that you're looking at me sort of through your lashes. It's very effective. Sugared or unsugared?"

Elizabeth lifted her chin, blinked. "Pardon me?"

"The iced tea. Sugared or unsugared?"

"Oh, sugar or no sugar? They're both no sugar. *Unsugared* isn't a word, I don't think, or at least not what is considered to be a good one. Not that I should have corrected you. I'm sorry. Richard is always making up new words, and I have to look them all up and then change them."

Will added two packets of sugar to his cup and then put the lid back on it. "You'd go crazy if you worked for me. Lawyers make up new words all the time. So what's in the bags?"

"I bought a new outfit for tonight," Elizabeth said before she could think up a suitable lie. "I also was talking to the lady in the shoe department, and she suggested a movie for us to see." She rested her elbow on the table and her chin in her palm. "Do you know something? I haven't been out shopping without the boys in, well, I can't remember when. It was heaven. They're too old now to come into the dressing room with me and too young to be left floating around on their own." She leaned back in her chair once more. "So thank you."

Will picked up his napkin and leaned in closer to her as he touched it to her chin. "Just a little pizza sauce. It looks good on you, though."

Elizabeth's breath caught in her throat. "Thank you, again."

He didn't move away. What moved away was the world. The food court, the noise, even her two sons, who had made remarkable inroads on the veggie pizza and were now competing with each other to see who could make the most noise with their straws as they sucked down the last of their lemonade.

What was left of Elizabeth's world was Will, so handsome in his silly baseball shirt, so young and vital and overwhelmingly male.

"This is nice," he said quietly. "Crazy but nice. But if I don't let you go home I won't be able to pick you up there later so that we can really be alone."

"You…you're doing it again," she pointed out, unable to shift her gaze away from his. "You're flirting."

His smile was like a punch to her stomach. "Yes, I know. How am I doing?"

"You're doing rather…rather well, actually. I think you've probably had a lot of practice."

"Ouch," Will said, sitting back at last. "Boys? I think I've just been sent to my room."

"Huh?" Mikey asked, looking at Will as if he'd just grown another head. "Mom said so? How can she say so? She's not your mom. She's *our* mom."

"Yes," Will said as they gathered up the empty cups and napkins and the pizza box and headed for the closest trash can, "but men always listen to women."

"But why?" Danny asked in all seriousness. Danny was often serious when he believed *rules* were involved. Mikey only learned the rules so he could know when he was breaking them.

"Yes, Will. Why?" Elizabeth asked. "I really want to hear this answer."

"All right," he said as they proceeded to the exit. "Here's the deal, boys. We men always listen to women because we're gentlemen, and it's polite."

"Oh. *That.* Mom says that all the time," Mikey said, unimpressed.

Will leaned closer to Elizabeth and whispered, "I could have told him a gentleman also gets farther with sugared rather than *unsugared,* but I figured he's still too young for that one."

"And yet nobody wonders why men still are allowed to rule the world," she whispered back at him. But then she smiled, because they were outside again, in the bright June sun, and the clouds were white as sugar against a gorgeous blue sky. She believed, really needed to believe, that Jamie was up there somewhere looking down at her and saying, "Well, it's about damn time, Liz. Welcome back to the world!"

Chapter Six

Will grabbed a towel to sling around his waist as he stepped out of the shower to hear his bedroom phone ringing. He had a momentary thought—all right, a momentary slap of panic—wondering if it might be Elizabeth phoning to cancel. He had pushed things a bit over lunch. Probably pushed too far…and he'd been beating himself up over it ever since, especially since he'd sworn to himself that tonight would be the last date. All right, maybe not *sworn*.

Although, she did seem to know how to push back. She'd even seemed to be enjoying herself.

"Hello," he said as he slammed down hard on Speaker before the call could go to his answering machine. He could talk Elizabeth out of canceling their date, he was sure of that. But you can't wheedle an answering machine message.

"Do you have me on Speaker? I *hate* being put on Speaker. It's like I'm talking to a mob in an echo chamber or something."

He sat down on the side of the bed. "What do you want, Chessie? You got me out of the shower."

"Good. Not as good as getting you out of bed at midnight, but I'll take it. I'm calling because I want to know what in the heck you were talking about last night."

"You don't remember?"

"Of course I remember. I just want to know why *you* don't know what you were talking about last night, that's all. I'm pretty sure you didn't. And then I want to know how Elizabeth managed to put you upside down on your head, because I may want to try it someday."

"And people wonder why you aren't married," Will teased, and then immediately flinched. "Ah, babe, I'm sorry. That was supposed to be a joke."

"No, my almost-trip down the aisle—*that* was a joke. Don't worry about it. You're a lawyer. You can't help but say stupid things."

"And what is that supposed to mean?"

"Hey, you tell me. I'm not the one working off a contempt of court charge. But seriously, Will, have I created a problem for you? I didn't mean to."

Will assured her he was fine, Elizabeth was fine, the whole damn world was just one big bowl of cherries.

The two hung up when the bell over the door of Second Chance Bridal rang and Chessie was called away to wait on a customer.

"Saved by the bell," Will said, getting to his feet.

Which saved him from having to tell Chessie she was right. Except that he wasn't just upside down on his head. He was also in too deep, out of his depth and pretty sure he was sinking. Fast.

Elizabeth walked into the boys' bedroom, noticing how the heels of her new shoes click-clicked rather satisfyingly on the old broad-cut wooden floor. "Okay, boys, I think you're all set. The movie you wanted is in the machine, so all you have to do is press Play. I put a box of microwave popcorn on the counter next to the microwave, and Elsie will make it when you're ready. Elsie isn't going to fall for any tall tales about your bedtime, and she will watch while you brush your teeth, so don't just try wetting the toothbrush and sticking it back in the holder. She raised three kids of her own, and you won't be able to fool her. Got that?"

"Mike does that, not me," Danny protested as he pushed his newly shorn and freshly washed hair through the neck hole of his superhero pajamas. Without the tube of slicker gel, his curls were back, but now they were tamed and ended at his nape. He looked at her, batting those eyes that were so much like his father's, and rubbed at his squeaky-clean shiny little nose. "Wow. You look good, Mom. All grown up."

Mikey, who had been picking up toys and tossing them into the wicker baskets lined up on a low shelf, paused in midthrow and looked at his mother. "Where's your hair?"

Elizabeth touched a hand to her nape. She'd debated for ten minutes but finally had decided to wear her hair up tonight. She thought it gave her neckline a good line. "You don't like it?"

Mikey shrugged. "It's all right."

"No, it's not. You're right, Mikey. Too stiff, too formal. It's dinner and a movie, not a night at the opera."

"What's an opera?" Danny asked her as he fingered the long necklace that hung nearly to her waist. "Are these real?"

"No, Danny. It's costume jewelry."

"You're wearing a *costume?*" the literal Mikey squeaked. "Who are you pretending to be?"

Elizabeth grinned as she pointed a finger at him. "Good question, Mikey. I'll let you know the minute I figure it out. Now, finish up in here, please. Elsie and Mr. Hollingswood will be here any minute."

"He says to call him Coach. He says William J. Hollingswood is only to impress the jury. What's a jury?"

"You two are, that's who," Elizabeth said, pulling pins from her hair as the doorbell rang. "Go get that, will you, please. I have to comb my hair."

Danny ran out of the room, heading for the door, but Mikey stayed where he was, his head tipped as he looked at his mother. Then he nodded. "That's better, Mom. You look real pretty." Then he surprised her by hugging her tightly around the waist, his damp, curly head making a slight water mark just beneath her breasts, before running after his brother.

Elizabeth's bottom lip trembled, and she bit it between her teeth as a memory came flashing back at her. Mikey had always liked to slide his chubby little fingers into her hair when she was feeding him his bottle. He'd tangle his hand in its length and then rub some strands between his fingers. She doubted he even remembered. He'd been so young. But she did.

She heard Elsie's voice in the kitchen and knew Will would soon arrive. Her heels click-clicked against the wooden floor as she retreated to the bathroom to comb her hair. Her hands were shaking. Only a little, but they were shaking.

"Stop it," she told her reflection. "It's just a date. You've been on dates before." *With Jamie, your steady boyfriend since the middle of tenth grade*, her brain, which seemed to be a stickler for accuracy this evening, reminded her. *Before that there was only Zachary Goobins, who took you to the fair and then lost you on the Midway, and David Hooker, who you slapped when he tried to get to second base…and you didn't even know what second base was.*

This would be the first time she would be with Will without having the twins along to act as a buffer. To act as chaperones. It was going to be just the two of them. What would they talk about? Would there be long, awkward silences? Would she try to fill them with stupid babbling? Would he try to kiss her good night? After all, the twins had eaten the last of the peanut butter cookies.

The doorbell sounded again, and the comb fell from Elizabeth's nerveless grip, clanking against the top of the sink. "Get a grip, woman," she ordered herself tersely. She stepped back from the vanity sink, turned from side to side to see if her underwear lived up to its promise—it did, no panty lines—and then touched her hand to the vague damp spot on the front of her dress.

How do you tell your child not to hug you? You don't!

She grabbed the hair dryer and held it a few inches from her dress as she watched the spot disappear without leaving any evidence—thank God Mikey had also decided against the hair gel after his shower.

Elizabeth returned to her bedroom to pick up the small purse and then walked to the window, to look out at the slowly setting sun. "Jamie? I know what you told me. I know what you wanted for me after you were gone, how unselfish you were. I was the selfish one. I didn't want to say goodbye. I didn't want to be alone. I was so afraid. I'm still afraid, Jamie. I'm afraid of so many things. But I'm never afraid that I will forget you."

She pressed her hands against her cheeks, feeling the burn of her flushed skin.

"Mom! Hey, Mom, Coach is here. He says he wants to see your costume."

"Oh, God." Elizabeth smiled out at the sun. "Stop laughing, Jamie. They're your sons, too, remember. As long as I have them, I have you."

* * *

She looked good enough to eat, Will decided as he walked down the outside stairs ahead of her and led the way to his car. Still wholesome, still all-American girl, still a mom. But there was an added extra something else tonight.

Those great legs that were even greater thanks to the way her high heels gave even more curve to her calves.

The bright pink dress skimmed her body in a way that demurely hinted rather than exploited, exposed. Which was, he'd decided within a nanosecond of seeing her walk into the kitchen, sexier than if the dress had been cut-down-to-there and slit-up-to-there glow-in-the-dark spandex.

He opened the car door for her but then blocked her entrance. "You know what? There's something we ought to get over with now, so we both aren't thinking about it all night."

She lifted a hand to her cheek, to push away the shiny, sleek hair that had blown slightly across her face in the soft evening breeze, and he fought the urge to do it for her, just so that he could touch her hair.

"I don't have a curfew, if that's what you're thinking. Elsie's going to stay overnight, sleep on the pull-out couch."

"She doesn't mind?"

Elizabeth shook her head, her gaze suddenly sliding away from his. "Elsie keeps her opinions to herself."

"More people should, and the world would be a happier place. But that's not what I was thinking about. We, well, *I,* left something unfinished last night. Do you know what that is?"

Her smile knotted a fist inside his chest. "Are you saying you really didn't come back for another peanut butter cookie?"

"Elsie's making more for me tomorrow," he told her. "But it wasn't the cook I was thinking about kissing. In fact, I've been thinking about kissing you ever since I left here last night. Which is why I thought we'd get it out of the way now, or I won't remember what we eat for dinner or anything about the movie. So what do you say? Should we get it over with?"

"Like a visit to the dentist sort of get it over with?"

"God, I hope not. But now you've got me worried. You're a lousy kisser?" he teased, lightly cupping the back of her neck in his hand.

"I'd like to think I'm just more of a slightly out-of-practice kisser," she said, her gaze meeting his unblinkingly.

He drew her closer. "Don't worry. It's probably like riding a bike. You never really forget…"

He lightly touched his lips to hers, expecting to be mildly pleased, because he liked kissing women, and he was pretty good at it. What he did not expect was to feel the near electric shock of awareness, of sweet, hot desire that instantly burned through him.

He could hold her forever, kiss her forever, draw himself inside her and her inside of him, making them one in a way that had little to do with sex and so very much more to do with being *home*. Being somewhere that he belonged, really belonged.

Visions of white picket fences danced in his head. Sunday barbecues, a swing set in a backyard filled with flowers. Baseball games and Christmas trees with shiny new bicycles sitting in front of them. Frolicking puppies and the smell of roast beef coming from the kitchen, and someone to kiss him hello and be really glad to see him...

Will put his hands on her shoulders and lightly pushed himself away from her, doing his best to smile down into her face, when what he really should be doing was heading for the airport and a flight to somewhere with topless beaches and assorted beauties of flexible morals, so he could remember what he really wanted out of life.

"Well, now that we've taken care of that," he said, hoping he didn't sound manic. "Now onward and upward, to my favorite Italian restaurant."

She looked as dazzled as he felt. Or was that only wishful thinking on his part?

"Oh, I get it now," Elizabeth said as she slipped into the front seat and looked up at him. "You're afraid I'll order everything with extra garlic on it."

"If you will, I will. That way we'll cancel each other out."

"And we won't have to worry about anyone sitting too close to us in the movie theater. Do you always plan ahead like this?"

"Absolutely," he said, before closing the door and

walking around the back of the Mercedes, where he dropped his keys, something he never did, and then smacked his knee on the bumper when he bent down to pick them up. At sixteen he'd had more finesse than this. Hell, when he was Dan and Mike's age he'd had more finesse than this. Where was his confidence? Where was the smooth operator who lived well, had never seen himself as the sort of man who wanted to be tied down? Women were fun. He enjoyed women. A lot. But all without strings, dammit. There would be plenty of time for strings when he was, oh, forty or so. If ever, because he liked his life.

He didn't like kids. He didn't like commitment. And he hated white picket fences!

There were no awkward silences over dinner, although Elizabeth didn't realize that, as she was too busy laughing and asking and answering questions, learning things about Will the not-always-obedient son, Will the not-always-serious college student, Will the maybe-sometimes-too-dedicated lawyer.

In turn, she'd told him about her own childhood, that she'd been captain of the baton twirling squad in high school, that her father had passed away unexpectedly only two weeks after she'd graduated, so that she'd stayed home from college to be with her mother and then, two years later, to marry Jamie.

The conversation turned more serious then, as they sat over coffee and dessert, and the show time for the last movie slipped past with neither of them noticing.

"Jamie was still in school—he was accepted to move up to the main campus at Penn State by his junior year, so I went with him to a small apartment in Happy Valley." She smiled at the memory, although it was easier to look back on those two years than to have to relive them again. "We were on the third floor, stuck between a party-hearty group of five male students below us and a herd of elephants in the apartment above us. Seriously," she said when Will smiled. "Elephants on pogo sticks, Jamie would say. And they never slept, which meant the twins never slept. The laundry was in another building, there was no elevator and I think we owned two pots and one frying pan. Jamie was in class all day, worked a part-time job on the weekends and studied at the library every night. Nobody could study with the twins around, and when the twins finally went to bed—"

"Let me guess. That's when the elephant pogo stick derby started," Will supplied, digging his spoon into the bowl of lemon sherbet and holding it up to her mouth.

"Mmm, that's so good," she said, accepting his offer and only a moment later realizing that his offer and her acceptance had seemed quite natural. "Anyway, it was a crazy couple of years. Nobody expects to have to grow up quite that fast, but we managed it."

"And as one of the guys who did more than his share of party-heartying in college, I apologize most profusely. I skidded through college on my charm, I admit, and only buckled down once I got to law school. I'm trying to picture that time and add a wife and two babies into the mix.

I can't imagine it. Plus, and don't hate me for this, I was a trust-fund baby, as well as on a full scholarship."

"Full scholarship? I thought you said you skidded through college."

"Not an academic scholarship, Elizabeth. I played baseball. I don't know how The Hammer knew that, but she got me good."

"I don't know. I've watched you, and I think you're enjoying yourself. I know Mikey and Danny think you're the best coach ever—and that's a quote."

"Pushing aside the fact that they've never had a coach before, I'll consider that a compliment." He waved to the waiter, who brought the check. "We've missed the movie, you know. What do you say we go walk off some of this meal instead? The parks are closed for the night, but there's a nice walking trail that runs through my condo development."

Elizabeth gave a quick thought to her new heels, which looked a lot better than they felt, but then nodded her agreement anyway. The night was feeling special, and if she'd said no, he might just take her home. She wasn't ready to go home.

Will's condo complex wasn't at all what Elizabeth envisioned, which was a series of apartment buildings divided up into residences. Instead, Will drove between decorative low brick walls marking the entrance to a community of two-story single homes, each house different in design but alike in its "accessories" of cream-colored stucco and red barrel-tile roofs.

The houses were well spaced, and the lawns were all

lush and deeply green. The roads were fairly narrow and curvy, with no sidewalks, and she could see that many of them ended in culs-de-sac complete with center islands planted with roses and small evergreens. It was all very beautiful…yet rather sterile.

"Pretty," she said as Will pulled the Mercedes into a double-wide driveway in front of a double-door garage that was painted brick-red, just like all the other garage doors.

"Is it? Sometimes I feel like the modern-day version of *The Stepford Wives*. Everything perfect. Matching but not matching and yet all still so oppressively the same. I nearly got brought up on the association's idea of federal charges last year when I tried hanging out a Philadelphia Eagles football banner. It interfered with the architectural concept, you understand. Which, by definition, I believe is Neo Classical Bland. You don't see the For Sale sign because they aren't allowed, either, but I do have the place on the market. Turns out I'm not the march in lockstep kind of guy who fits in here."

"But you bought the house, I mean the condo. So there must have been a time you thought you were a…a lockstep kind of guy."

"What can I say, the place comes with a great golf course and some pretty cool clay tennis courts. I just didn't count on anyone really taking all the condo restrictions seriously. Then I met Mrs. Thorogood. I've met Mrs. Thorogood a lot, actually, in this past year. *You're in my black books again, Mr. Hollingswood*," he sing-songed, waving his finger in Elizabeth's face. *"White lights only for Christmas decoration, Mr. Hollingswood, and no crass commercial decorative figures on the communal lawn.* I ended up with Santa Claus waving at me from my foyer. It just wasn't the same. All this, and the condo association fees seem to go up every month. Secretly, I think they're pooling together to hire a lawyer who can figure out how to get me out of here."

Elizabeth laughed as they got out of the car and stood together on the driveway. "People actually *pay* to be told what to do in their own homes? That's horrible."

"No, it's what they want. The condos supposedly sell after only a few days on the market. Mine's been on for a week now, and I've already received two offers. I figure one more is the charm, and then I'll pick one of them to be the lucky people who get to not put out their Santa next Christmas." He took her hand. "Come on, the path is just down here at the end of the street. Let's walk."

Elizabeth sighed inwardly as they walked along the side of the narrow roadway, caught between the peaceful quiet of the evening and the tingling awareness of the man who walked beside her. Holding her hand. Pointing out the condo where Mrs. Thorogood resided, joking with her that, although each lawn was well manicured, somehow it always looked as if the blades of grass in Mrs. Thorogood's front yard all stood at attention.

When they reached the macadam path, Elizabeth

asked him to stop and then used him as a supporting prop as she slipped out of her heels. "Ah, that's better. I'm much more used to sandals and sneakers, I'm afraid. Do you mind?"

"Not if you don't," he said, taking her shoes from her and holding them by the heel straps as they continued down the path. "This should be a beach, and we could wade in the ocean as a full moon makes a pathway across the water. Since it isn't, would you settle for a walk along the fourteenth fairway? The grass has to be softer than this macadam, and there are a few sand traps and a pond near the green, so we can pretend we're at the beach."

"We're allowed on the course at night?"

He laughed softly. "I'll put it this way. If we see a rather large woman wearing a pink polka-dot dress and a look of outraged dignity advancing toward us—well, it's every man for himself."

"You'd desert me and run away?"

"No, I suppose not. It would probably be safer to hide behind you. I don't think she'd hit another woman."

"You're making that up. Mrs. Thorogood never hit you."

"No, but she's thought about it. Did I tell you about the skunks?"

Somehow they'd gone from hand in hand to arm in arm, probably because he thought she might stumble in the dark now that they'd left the pretty lights of the walking trail behind them. Now she looked around her nervously. "No, I don't think you've mentioned skunks."

"Matt Peters, my partner in the law firm—Hollingswood and Peters, Attorneys At Law, you know, very classy—thought it would be fun to hire this company that puts creatures in your front yard to celebrate your birthday. Well, flamingos, cows, buzzards or whatever the heck else they use. One for each year. Matt, who thinks he's so clever, went for skunks. Cardboard skunks, thirty-two of them, one for each year. Along with a sign that read *Getting Old Stinks*."

"Let me guess. Mrs. Thorogood was not amused."

"Mrs. Thorogood physically pulled every damn last one of those skunks out of the ground and threw them on my porch."

Elizabeth laughed. "Oh, she did not."

"Oh, but she did. I've got video of the whole thing. It's beautiful. I'll show it to you some time. Whoops. Steady there. Step in a hole?"

Elizabeth kept her left foot off the ground as she clung to him. "No, it was a rock or something. I'm probably fine."

He peered at the ground. "Damn. Not a rock, a concrete yard marker. I doubt you care, but it means we're one hundred and fifty yards from the green." And then, before she could protest, he'd scooped her up in his arms and was walking back toward the path. "There's benches every so often, under the lights. We can see the damage better."

Elizabeth clung to him—really, was there anything

else she could do? The man had picked her up, for goodness' sake. "I'm fine, Will, really. It was just...unexpected."

He headed toward the nearest light lining the path, and there was a bench sitting beneath it, just as if he'd ordered it to be there. "I'll put you down, but keep your foot up until we can see what you did."

"*I* didn't do anything," she pointed out as he lowered her on her right foot and then held on to her as she eased down onto the bench. "I didn't even twist my ankle. I'm fine."

"Ya-huh," he said, reaching down to take hold of her calf and lift her leg, which sent her to quickly holding down the skirt of her dress. "Oh, boy, you're bleeding."

"I am?" Elizabeth leaned forward in surprise, the better to see her foot. "Where? I don't feel like I'm bleeding. I mean, I don't hurt or anything. How much blood?"

"That depends. How squeamish are you?"

"I've got two seven-year-olds who think falling down and running into things is their job. One more trip to the local walk-in clinic and they'll start keeping a file on me," Elizabeth muttered, trying to bend her leg so that she could see the sole of her foot. But Will was holding tight to her heel and wouldn't let go. "I'm not going to faint, Will."

"That's good to know. It's not horrible, but you can't walk on it barefoot on this macadam, either. Let's get you back to the house."

"I can hop," Elizabeth protested, having already decided that her first date in a decade or more was not exactly going to be one she would share details of with Chessie during any girl-talk session. "Really, Will, I can—never mind," she said as, once again, he picked her up as if she weighed no more than one of the twins. "Wait, my shoes. They're on the bench."

"So? I thought they hurt your feet."

"But...but they're pretty," she said, knowing how silly that sounded.

Will turned back to the bench and then bent his knees so that she was low enough to be able to reach the shoes. "So are tigers, but I wouldn't advise trying to pet one."

"Oh, good logic. I'm bleeding, and the man gives me logic. I'm really bleeding? Because I still don't feel anything."

"You're probably in shock," Will told her matter-of-factly as they left the trail and were headed back up the street to his condo. "Put your head on my shoulder. That should help. That, and I've got some brandy that'll get your heart pumping again."

"Oh, really," Elizabeth said, the light from the street-lamp revealing the smile on Will's face...and the twinkle in his eyes. "Exactly how much blood is there?"

"You're doubting me?"

"I'm beginning to, yes," she told him just as a porch light went on and a door opened at the condo with the at-attention grass blades.

"*Mis-ter* Hollingswood! What do you think you're doing with that young woman?"

"I swear to God she sits at her window 24/7, just so she can leap out at people," Will grumbled, stopping to turn toward the clearly disapproving Mrs. Thorogood. "Well, hi there, neighbor. Look what I found on the golf course. I'm going to take her home with me now and ply her with liquor. Have a nice evening!"

Elizabeth bit her lips between her teeth and buried her head against the side of Will's neck to smother her giggles.

"Well, that got her back in her cave," Will said as he continued along the road, crossing his yard and only putting Elizabeth down when he'd reached his front porch. "Then again, she could be calling the police. I should have thought of that one."

"You're insane. Do you know that?" Elizabeth asked him as he opened the door and then led her, hopping, into the condo. "That poor old woman."

"That poor old woman can pull staked skunks from the ground with one hand and flip them twenty feet onto a porch. I've got video, remember? Can you hop from here?"

"To where?" Elizabeth asked him as he turned on the lights and she saw a long, wide hallway made up of a deep cherrywood floor, creamy wainscoted walls and a marvelous tray ceiling, the center of which was painted a lush cranberry. As she looked further she could see that a dining area had been carved out of the space and marked by white wooden columns. "Where's your kitchen?"

"Straight ahead, past the stairs. I'm going to go upstairs and find my first aid kit."

The moment he was gone, Elizabeth leaned a hand against the wall to balance herself and bent her leg so she could get a look at this horrible bleeding wound she couldn't even feel.

"Oh, ouch. Okay, *now* it hurts." She must have stepped on the very edge of the marker and then sort of slid down it, because the scrape went from the middle of her arch and ran straight up toward the top of her foot. It wasn't a cut, not really, but more of a three-inch long brush burn that had only bled in a couple of places. Mikey's latest boo-boo had looked much the same last week when he'd tripped over his shoelace and gone down on the driveway, skinning his knee.

Gingerly, she put her foot down, keeping her weight on her toes, and made her way into the kitchen just as Will joined her, holding a white plastic box with a red cross on it.

She sank onto a chair at the table and waved at the box. "Let me guess, you were a Boy Scout." She noticed that he'd taken off his sports coat and removed his tie. She admired him when he was more formal, but he was so much more approachable like this. Still the most handsome man she'd ever seen but more human than Greek god.

"Hey, don't knock it. If Mrs. Thorogood comes bursting in here, I could tie her up using six different knots." He pulled out another chair and motioned for her to rest her foot on it. "Okay, not as bad as it looked earlier, but you lost some skin, didn't you? Are you up to date on your tetanus shots?"

"Yes, Dr. Will," Elizabeth said, wondering why she hadn't already sunk into a hole somewhere in embarrassment. "Look, it's really not all that bad. If you'd just wet a couple of paper towels, I'll wash it off and—"

Will shot her a look that told her she'd probably be smart to just sit back and let him play doctor, so she did.

From his back pocket, he produced a washcloth he'd brought downstairs with him, and for the next five minutes she watched in varying degrees of embarrassment and then rather disturbing awareness as he tended to her injury.

He held her calf cupped in one hand as he carefully washed her foot, as he knelt in front of her and checked to make sure there were no bits of grass or grit in the wound, and, finally, as he used a cotton swab to spread antibiotic ointment on it, then taped a gauze pad to her foot.

It was all very mundane…and all very intimate, devastatingly personal.

"Extremely professional," she said as he patted the last strip of tape in place. "Clearly you're a man of many talents. Thank you. And, um, you can let go of my leg and get up now, since you're probably not planning to propose."

His expression turned serious as he took hold of her hands and helped her to her feet. "You have no idea what all I could propose right now. Elizabeth…"

She looked up at him, seeing the question in his eyes, knowing hers were probably just as full of questions for him. "It…um…it's been a very long time," she said at last, knowing he understood what she meant, just as she'd understood what he'd meant.

He ran his hands up and down her bare arms as he nodded. "I know. And I was fully prepared to take advantage of that. I'm not the nicest guy in the world, Elizabeth. I can be pretty ruthless when it comes to getting what I want."

"I don't know what I want," she told him, trading honesty for honesty. "I feel…I feel like I've been asleep for a very long time. Part of me, anyway. The part that wants. The part that—*you know?* How would you know that?" She turned away from him, hugging herself protectively. "Is there some invisible tattoo on my forehead or something, Will, that only men can read? Widow, hasn't had any for a while, bound to be very grateful—is that what it says?"

He didn't answer her, not at once, but only put his hands on her shoulders, kneading her suddenly tense muscles.

"You have two kids, yet you look so—all right, I'll say it. Virginal. You look virginal. Untouched, like some sleeping princess in a fairy tale. I'm a man, Elizabeth. One look, and I knew I wanted to wake you up, rotten and premeditated and cold as that sounds, even to me."

Elizabeth sighed from her depths, allowing herself to lean back against his chest. "But not wrong. You wouldn't have been wrong. I'd be lying to you, as well as to myself, if I didn't say that I've thought about how this evening would end and…and if I was ready to…

live again, I guess." Then, her mind made up, she looked him steadily in the eye. "And now I know. The answer is yes. I'm ready."

Then once again she was lifted high against his chest, and he was carrying her back down the hallway, climbing the staircase as she held on tightly, praying she could let herself go.

His bedroom was all in shadows, with only the faint glow from the streetlight allowing her to make out the shapes of the furniture as he lowered her onto the bed, then followed her down.

His kisses were gentle, his touch slow and unhurried. It was as if with each kiss, each new intimacy, he was giving her time to change her mind, to say no.

But she couldn't say no. Not when her body was saying yes. Yes, hold me, touch me, remind me that there is a woman here. Not just a mother, not just the remembrance of young love, but a mature woman with wants, with needs. A woman who deserves to feel alive again, who has been asleep much too long, only going through the motions, yet not really alive.

He kissed away her clothing, bit by tantalizing bit, the night air cool against her fevered skin. He didn't take. He gave, as if knowing just what she needed. There was no clumsiness about him, no indecision. There was none of the haste that turned foreplay into something to be done so that the ultimate prize could be gotten to as quickly as possible.

He made love slowly, thoroughly, lingering over her breasts until she thought she'd go mad, whispering how beautiful she was, how good she felt to him, how very perfect she was, in every way.

And she believed him. She needed to believe him, so she did. She needed to feel free, unfettered and even vaguely powerful. She dared to touch him, to run her fingertips over the soft mat of hair on his chest, aware of the muscles just below his skin.

By the time he slid his hand between her thighs she was ready for him, more than ready for him, and the soft explosions that rocked her would have been embarrassing if he hadn't kept his hand against her sex protectively even as he whispered in her ear. "Yes, Elizabeth. You need this. Let go, sweetheart. Let go…"

"I'm…" She was having trouble regaining her breath. "I'm sorry…"

"I'm not," he said, his face inches from hers, his hand already moving against her, his fingers sliding easily inside her. "We're only just getting started…"

He made love to every inch of her. With his hands, with his mouth. With teeth and tongue, he brought her to a new awareness of her wants and needs. With words that soothed, inflamed, teased and aroused her. He took liberties she would not have imagined, and she didn't just let him. She was an active participant, daring her own intimate explorations, her passion feeding on his, her responses heightened when he moaned his pleasure at her touch.

He kissed the bandage on her foot, the surprisingly responsive skin behind her knee. His hands gently kneaded her inner thighs before he lifted her legs up and over his shoulders and applied all his considerable talents to introducing her to delights she had no idea existed.

There was no right. There was no wrong. There was only Will, only pleasure, only the moment. She was achingly, thrillingly, mind-blowingly alive.

As the ripples of yet another orgasm cascaded through her, he at last gave her what she wanted most of all. To be filled up with him, to feel him close inside her, driving her, taking her deeper, faster, higher. And when at last she felt the spasms of his release, she held on to him tightly, glorying in his passion, nearly laughing out loud with the pure joy of feeling again.

Chapter Seven

The bell above the doorway at Second Chance Bridal rang as Elizabeth stepped into the shop at precisely noon on the day after her rebirth. That's how she was looking at the thing, as a rebirth. She was alive again, thanks to Will. It was a good feeling.

"Hey there, Elizabeth," Chessie said, coming out from the area of the dressing rooms. "Is it noon already? So glad there was no problem changing our dinner to lunch." Then she stopped, cocked her head to one side as she looked at her. "There's something different about you today," she said, frowning. "You look…okay, different, it's probably safer settling for different. Looks good on you, though."

"Thanks," Elizabeth said, feeling her cheeks

growing hot. She knew what Chessie meant, because she had seen it for herself this morning in her bathroom mirror. Her eyes seemed brighter, more aware of her surroundings. Her skin had almost a glow about it.

And she couldn't seem to stop smiling. Which was probably a dead giveaway to someone as astute as she was pretty sure Chessie was.

"Do you want to visit your gown?"

"Hmm?" Elizabeth said, really not paying attention, as she relived Will's good-night kiss at the bottom of the steps for at least the thousandth time. He'd kissed her at least a half dozen times, as if reluctant to let her go. As if they had found, shared, much more than sex.

But she'd been ready to say good-night to him, because she'd wanted to go upstairs, snuggle beneath the covers and grin until her cheeks ached. She'd wanted to stuff the corner of her pillow in her mouth so that she could giggle like a teenager. She'd wanted to climb onto the roof outside her window and shout to the world: I'm here! I'm alive!

She should send the man flowers. That's what she should do.

"Elizabeth? Yoo-hoo, Earth to Elizabeth. I said, do you want to visit your gown?"

"Oh," Elizabeth said, bringing herself back to attention. Really, she had to stop daydreaming. She'd poured orange juice on Danny's cereal this morning, for goodness' sake. And he'd *liked* it, which just went to show what seven-year-olds knew about haute cuisine.

"Uh-oh, the smile's gone. It's not your magical gown anymore?"

"Oh, no, it's a gorgeous gown. I just…I just think I'm most likely minus a groom."

Chessie rubbed her palms together, seemed to realize what she was doing, and quickly dropped her hands to her sides. "Really? Did you and your Richard have an argument? And how would you do that, long-distance?"

"Chicago. He's in Chicago, or maybe he left for Denver this morning. I'm not sure. But Richard doesn't know," Elizabeth said, collapsing into one of the chairs flanking the fireplace now fronted by a huge vase of fresh-faced daisies in a golden pot, and looking up at Chessie imploringly. "You're going to have to help me figure out a way to tell him."

"Uh-huh," Chessie said, her huge cornflower-blue eyes looking vaguely panicked, as if good news had suddenly turned troubling. "Hold that thought, okay? I need to go in the back and make a quick call."

While her new friend was gone, Elizabeth picked up one of the bridal magazines fanned out on a small table and began paging through it. The gowns were all beautiful. So were the displays of china and stemware and jewelry. But what caught and held her attention were the pages and pages toward the back of the magazine that were filled with suggested honeymoon spots all over the world.

Mostly, she was intrigued with the photo spread of various vacation spots in the Caribbean. Beautiful waterfront hotels, each more glamorous than the other.

Why, she and the boys could even swim with dolphins if they wanted to—what fun! And they were old enough now to really enjoy themselves on a vacation that didn't include amusement parks and people dressed up like chipmunks.

"My first real vacation," Elizabeth said softly, running her hand over the page, already mentally packing suitcases.

"Okay, my call went straight to voicemail, but I left a message," Chessie said, stomping back into the reception area. "He'll call back if he knows what's good for him."

"I wouldn't call back if you used that tone in your message," Elizabeth told her, shutting the magazine. "Did somebody screw up an order, or something?"

Chessie coughed, almost choked. "Yes, I think you could say that. But he'll make it right, because he knows I'd skin him alive if he didn't. Are you ready? Marylou can't come, darn it. She's off on one of her tangents again. She's always got some sort of project going. But Eve is going to meet us at the restaurant. And get ready, because she's going to ask you to have a couple of her books autographed. Turns out she's a huge Richard Halstead fan. Now, not another word about this seeming epiphany you've had about Richard until we get to the restaurant, or Eve will just make you repeat everything anyway. She's very nosy."

"But you're not? Maybe you don't want me to tell you?" Elizabeth said, preceding Chessie onto the porch and waiting as she turned over the Closed sign and locked the door.

"Yeah, right, like I'm not dying to hear every single detail," Chessie said, grinning at her. "I just think I might need a glass of wine to go with the telling."

Will climbed the stairs to Elizabeth's apartment, still second-guessing his purchase of two official IronPigs replica home team jerseys for the boys. But flowers didn't seem like the right note. Maybe too personal a gesture, one that said things neither of them had said last night or probably wanted to think about too much today. Still, he hadn't wanted to show up empty-handed, so a trip to the store at the ballpark had seemed a good idea at the time.

His cell phone vibrated in his pocket, but he let the call go to his voicemail and knocked on the door, rehearsing his big hello and his offer to give the twins a little fielding practice, since the team practice had been canceled this morning thanks to a conflict with another team wanting to use the field.

Danny opened the door, not looking at Will, but with his head turned, calling over his shoulder, "Mom did too say I could have one! Ask Aunt Elsie. She'll tell you! Oh, hi, Coach. Mom's not home."

"Oh? Is she up at the house, working?"

Danny shook his head. "No, she went to have lunch somewhere with her friend. Jessie?"

Will didn't know what it felt like to have a goose walk over your grave, but suddenly he thought he had a pretty good idea of the sensation. "Chessie?"

"Yeah, that's it. Jess—*Chessie.* And later we're all

going to go have hot dogs at Todd's house and then go miniature golfing. If Mikey cleans up his side of the room. I cleaned up mine, and *I* get a cupcake now, but *he* doesn't. Not until he puts all his junk away."

"Seems only fair. Hey, do you know where they're having lunch? Your mom and Chessie."

Danny shook his head. "Nope. I think it was supposed to be supper, but now it's lunch because we're going to Todd's house. What's in the bag?"

Will nearly hid the bag behind his back. "Uh, nothing. Just something I— Hey, I have an idea. How about I pick you guys up tomorrow, you and your mom, and we all go to Dorney Park? I hear they've opened up another waterslide, and then we can take in some of the rides?"

"We've never been to Dorney Park," Danny said, considering the offer. "We've seen the roller coasters from the highway when we go to the dentist, but Mom never took us to the park."

"Then maybe I should clear the idea first with your mother." Will wasn't used to this, the protocol of taking children along on his dates.

"Okay. I'm going to get my cupcake now. It's got sprinkles. Bye," Danny said, already closing the door.

"Yeah, bye. *Bon appétit,*" Will said to the closed door, smiling and shaking his head as he heard Danny's argument with his brother take up where it had left off. He went back down the steps, pulling his cell phone from his pocket as he walked to his car.

Two voicemail messages. Maybe one of them was

from Elizabeth? But, no, she didn't have his cell phone number. The calls had to be something to do with one of the cases he was working on.

Except they weren't.

The first message was from Kay Quinlan.

"Hi, stranger. Tired of playing Mr. Mom yet? Or should I say playing *with* Mom? I've got two orchestra seat tickets for the show at the State Theater tonight, and then we can go back to my place and get naughty. Call me."

He deleted the message, probably pressing Delete with more energy than strictly necessary, and brought up the second message:

"What did you do? What did I tell you? Do you remember what I told you? Wake her up, I said—not *light* her up, for crying out loud. Now she's going to call off the wedding. Okay, so maybe that's the best thing but not this way. You *idiot!* God only knows what she's thinking now, and God help her if she thinks *you're* some kind of Prince Charming who's come to her rescue, because we all know that when it comes to women, you have the attention span of a gnat. Call me!"

Will played the message again, and then a third time, just to be sure he understood what Chessie had said.

The wedding.

What wedding?

He punched in the numbers for his cousin's cell phone, but the call went straight to voicemail. He slammed the phone shut, not trusting himself to leave a message, and then barely restrained himself from flinging the thing toward the tennis courts.

What the hell was going on?

* * *

Elizabeth liked Eve the moment she first saw her. Fortyish, and with a twinkle in her bright blue eyes that advertised her obvious love of life, she had dark brown hair, cut short and feathered around her face, and when she smiled, deep dimples appeared in her cheeks. If Peter Pan had a sister, Eve would be perfect for the role, because within ten minutes of listening to her across the luncheon table, it was fairly certain that Eve D'Allesandro planned never to grow up.

They spoke of inconsequential things for a while, sort of feeling each other out, getting to know each other. Elizabeth laughed as she learned more about the absent Marylou, and she made Chessie promise to introduce them. And then, feeling comfortable, Elizabeth told them she had decided that marriage to Richard probably wasn't a good idea.

But before Chessie could respond—although she looked ready to pounce—Eve said, "I still can't believe Richard Halstead lives right here, in dinky old Allentown."

"Allentown is not dinky," Chessie reprimanded. "Besides, everyone has to live somewhere."

"True. But the Côte d'Azur seems more like it. Not Saucon Valley. Next you'll have Elizabeth here tell me that the man actually puts on his pants one leg at a time."

Elizabeth laughed. Clearly these two loved to argue. "How else would he do it, Eve? Have somebody else hold them up while he jumps off the roof and lands in them feet first?"

"I don't know, Chessie. It's just a saying."

"Yeah, well, it's a dumb saying. Writers are people, just like everyone else."

"Now you're just being depressing. I know he only writes about Jake LaRue—lordy, lordy, what a hero!— but I *want* to think he lives like him, too."

Elizabeth watched, her chin in her hand, as the two women bounced the conversation back and forth across the table. It was like a verbal tennis match. "I'm guessing I shouldn't tell you that Richard needs reading glasses, his favorite sweater has a hole in the elbow he won't let me fix and his most-loved food is pot roast."

Eve flung herself back in her chair. "Oh! Now all my illusions are shattered. And that's not really him on the book jacket? Or somebody airbrushed away two extra chins and huge bags under his eyes? Please don't tell me that."

"Richard is an extremely handsome man," Elizabeth told her, trying not to grin. "I'd say the photograph on his book covers doesn't do him justice. There, do you feel better now?"

"Immensely," Eve said, sitting forward once more and picking up her martini glass. "So, if you're not going to marry the guy, can I have him?"

"Eve, go to your room," Chessie said, shaking her head. "Elizabeth, ignore her. *Please* ignore her. Now, are you going to tell us why you've decided not to marry Richard?"

Elizabeth looked to Eve, and then back to Chessie. There was no way she was going to tell Chessie about what had happened last night with Will. No possible way. "I don't know exactly how to put this," she began tentatively. "I've just suddenly realized that *settling* is not an option for me. I thought it was, I believed it was…but it's not. There has to be more."

Eve popped a French fry into her mouth. "More what? Oh, wait a minute. I think I get it. He doesn't light your fire? How can that be? He sure lights mine, and I've only seen his picture."

Elizabeth looked at Chessie for help.

"Eve, that's pretty personal," Chessie said, shrugging, as if she didn't expect that to stop her friend, but, hey, she'd given it her best shot.

"Well, of course it's personal. You don't marry a man just because he's *there.*" Eve leaned forward, her elbows on the table. "Here's my rule of thumb, Elizabeth. If you can keep your hands off him, dump him."

"We're very compatible," Elizabeth said. "There's more to love than sex."

"Uh-huh, sure," Eve said, rolling her eyes. "So—what is it?"

"What is what?" Elizabeth asked, feeling Chessie's eyes on her.

"What is more important than sex?"

"Eve, she didn't say sex wasn't important. She said there's more to love than just an overpowering urge to jump someone's bones—oh, God, now I'm talking like you. I shouldn't have had that glass of wine."

"No, no, she's right," Elizabeth said, realizing that this was something else she'd been missing out on for too many years. Girl talk. "At least sort of right. I do love Richard. He's a wonderful, caring man. And then there's the boys. We'd be financially secure, which isn't a minor consideration in this day and age. There are so many good reasons our marriage could work. But—oh, Lord, how do I say this? But…but I'm not even thirty yet, you know? Is *comfortable* really what I should be looking for at this point in my life?"

"See? I told you. He doesn't light her fire. Doesn't ring her bells." Eve reached across the table and laid her hand on Elizabeth's. "I've got a good five or six years on you—"

"Try twelve," Chessie interrupted, toasting the air with her wineglass. "But do go on. We're hanging on your every word of wisdom, O Ancient One."

"Ignore her. She never drinks, and now you know why. What I'm saying is, I'm a few years older than you, and I know I'm still a long way from looking for somebody *comfortable*. I'll bet you Richard isn't, either. I mean, I read his books. Maybe Richard isn't getting any, but Jake LaRue sure is. Ergo, Richard wants it, too. It only makes sense."

"Jake LaRue saves the world and shoots people," Elizabeth reminded Eve. "Does that mean Richard wants to shoot people, too?"

"Back to you, O Ancient One," Chessie said, checking her cell phone for messages. "Ah, he called back.

Good. Now he can wait for me. Eve? You were saying something profound?"

"Yes, I know. But now I've lost my train of thought. Oh, right. No, Elizabeth, he doesn't want to shoot people. At least no more than any of us do."

Chessie, who had been in the midst of sipping from her water glass, had to quickly put the glass down and grab up her napkin to catch the dribbles. "No more than any of us do? You want to explain that one, killer?"

Eve glared at her. "Are you going to keep interrupting me? Because I'm trying to make a point here. I understand men. After all, I've been married, remember?"

"Yes, we know. Twice."

"Once! I keep telling you that the first one didn't count."

Elizabeth couldn't help herself. She felt the laugh begin low in her belly, and biting her bottom lip to keep it from exploding from her simply wasn't going to work. Her laughter poured from her, her new delight in life, in her new friends. Just the way she *saw* life at the moment was so delicious, so *freeing,* that she was soon giggling like the twins, laughing at silliness until tears rolled down her cheeks.

"That is one happy woman," Eve confided as Elizabeth tried in vain to control her case of the giggles. "You know what that means, don't you? She's getting some."

Chessie turned wide eyes toward Elizabeth, her expression one of such panic that all Elizabeth could do was nod her agreement with Eve before she went off in another paroxysm of pure unadulterated glee.

Chapter Eight

Elizabeth sat in the darkened living room, the only light coming from the television set and a show about what some committee of people who'd never scrubbed a bathroom floor on their hands and knees in their lives considered the top ten bathrooms in the country.

A shower stall without a door or curtain, but just open to the rest of the bathroom—*and* complete with handheld sprayers? What idiot thought that could work? It didn't take a genius to know the havoc Danny and Mikey could wreak with an arrangement like that. She'd have to build an ark.

A bathtub you could fill up to the very top and then even let the water run over the sides and into some reservoir or something? Who paid the water bill, for one thing? Had these people never heard about conserving natural resources, for another?

But most importantly—did none of the people who owned these Taj Mahal bathrooms have children? It had taken her nearly an hour to clean up the bathroom tonight after both boys had been bathed. How was it possible to get so dirty playing miniature golf?

Elizabeth did know how, however, as she'd watched. The boys had definitely found and become attached to every bit of dust and dirt they could on the course, not to mention the disaster that had been their rainbow-flavored water-ices that had been served up in double-size but flimsy paper cups that had begun to leak almost immediately. A little colored melting ice, a little dust, and *bam,* instant huge, sticky, grimy mess.

And she'd like to know how Mikey managed to get some of that mess *inside* his sneaker. Even with two bath towels put in with them, she could still hear the thump-thump of four size-five sneakers going round and round in the dryer.

But she'd had fun overall. The boys had been not only well behaved but actually quite amusing. They weren't babies anymore, but more like real people. And although he hadn't stopped at the apartment a second time, or even called and left a message while she was gone, the twins had told her that Will wanted to take them all to the waterslides at Dorney Park tomorrow.

How dirty could the twins get in a pool?

Life, by and large, was actually pretty good. Because she was finally allowing it to be pretty good, to be fun again, to not feel guilty when she smiled, or went a day without thinking about Jamie.

She'd had sex. No, she'd had great sex. And that had been fun, too.

Elizabeth had no thoughts about a long-term relationship with Will Hollingswood. She certainly wasn't thinking in terms of forever or shoes and rice and all of that. She doubted he was thinking along those lines, either.

And that was fine. That was good. Hopping into bed with the man couldn't by any stretch of the imagination be seen as taking baby steps back into life, but he'd shown her that there still was a life out there for her.

What she and Will had, if they could be said to have anything after only one night together, was an adult relationship. What she and Richard had—and they definitely did have something—was a mature relationship.

Clearly, if the way she'd been feeling all day could be used as a yardstick, an adult relationship beat a mature relationship, hands down.

Even if some of the bloom had gone off her euphoria since last night, and she was feeling a little sad that Will hadn't called her. He'd stopped by when she was out having lunch with Chessie and Eve, and that was nice, but that was also it. He hadn't tried to contact her again. She didn't think she'd disappointed him in bed. He certainly hadn't acted like a man who'd been disappointed.

Had she been too willing? After all, they barely knew each other.

Did it matter? Again, she wasn't looking for a husband. She already had one waiting in the wings if that was what she wanted, right?

Widowhood had been a cocoon—first one of necessity and then, probably, one of choice. It was safer in the cocoon, just her and her boys. But the twins were growing up; it wasn't as if she could stack bricks on their heads and keep them little, totally dependent on her, as she was on them.

So it had been time to emerge from the cocoon, to see if she could spread her new wings, be a butterfly. Will understood that; he was a man of the world.

Richard had offered her a bigger cocoon, that's all. Will offered her nothing but the sky. It was up to her what to do with it.

"You're not eighteen anymore," she told herself out loud. "You don't have to marry the man just because you slept with him. That's what adult relationships are all about."

Maybe it would be better if she simply didn't see Will again, outside the baseball practices and games, where she had to see him.

She took a deep breath and let it out on a sigh. Well, that thought had taken the rest of the air out of her brand-new balloon, hadn't it?

Elizabeth lifted the remote and pointed it toward the television, feeling she'd seen far enough into the lives of the rich and ridiculous, and began clicking through the channels.

Infomercial. The life cycle of the honeybee. Infomercial. She paused with her finger over the button to watch Lucy and Ethel work on an assembly line in a chocolate factory, smiling even though she'd seen that episode of *I Love Lucy* a thousand times. Then she moved on through three channels in a row, all dealing with true crimes, complete with gory details and a commentator who seemed much too cheerful to be talking about a guy hiring a hit man to kill his wife. Infomercial—this one for a tiny bit of plastic that supposedly hid your bra straps, gave you instant cleavage and relieved backaches. If you ordered now, you got two of them for the price of one.

"Which is still about five million times more than that bit of plastic cost to manufacture," she grumbled, wondering what was wrong with her. Usually she laughed at these things.

And she'd been so happy—no, slap happy—just ten hours ago in the restaurant with Chessie and Eve.

Maybe it was because Annie's husband had decided at the last minute to come along to the miniature golf course, which had made her feel like a third wheel, even with the boys so clearly enjoying themselves. Maybe it had been the way Todd Sr. had stood behind Annie and helped her time a putt that had to avoid the slowly rotating blades of a wooden windmill. Maybe it was the way the two of them teased and seemed to finish each other's sentences…and seemed so complete in one another.

Maybe, after an evening of glorious sex and an afternoon of wine and girlish giggles, she was lonely.

Maybe she missed Will. Not the sex. Will.

Suddenly she felt homesick for her cocoon. Life was easier when you didn't *feel*.

The phone rang, nearly sending her heart into her throat, and she grabbed at it even as she looked at the mantel clock to see it was past eleven. Phone calls after eleven at night or before eight in the morning were never good news. At times like this, "Who died?" was what she wanted to ask when she picked up the phone, even as she was saying a cautious hello.

"Elizabeth? You answered quickly. I was worried I might wake you."

"Richard?" Elizabeth cleared her mind of both bad thoughts about her mother maybe taking a header in her Florida kitchen and her secondary assumption—which was *then you're not Will?* and tried to slow her heartbeat. "No, I haven't gone to bed yet. Did you try to call earlier? Another mother from the baseball team and I took the boys out for a totally unhealthy dinner, and then we all went miniature golfing. Danny had a hole in six," she added, smiling. "It was his best hole of the night, and Mikey hit one ball over the—"

"Elizabeth, I'm coming home," Richard interrupted. "I'm already at the gate, and my plane boards in five minutes, so please excuse me for cutting you off. I have a driver picking me up at the airport, but I'd like you to be at the house when I arrive. I imagine Elsie can come over and stay with the boys if you think they shouldn't be alone."

Well, of course I can't leave them here alone, Elizabeth thought. And did he have to sound like this was some Mother Hen complex he disagreed with, or was she just overreacting? She adored Richard, but he did seem to believe he was the center of the universe.

Oops. And she was his employee. She'd forgotten that part for a moment. This wasn't Richard the maybe-fiancé speaking. This was her boss.

"Richard? Are you all right? Where are you, anyway?"

"Denver Airport, which is probably very nice, but I'd rather be on the plane, with someone offering me a pillow and blanket. And definitely a stiff drink, except that I'm already higher than the proverbial kite on pain meds and muscle relaxants, and clumsy as it seems I am, that's probably not a good idea."

"Clumsy, you? You're in pain? What happened? Did you fall?" Not her mother, then, but Richard. And her mother was only seven years older than Richard. And why was she suddenly thinking about *that?*

"Fell, tumbled, went ass over teacups—you name it, I did it. Getting out of the damn hotel shower, and I never did figure out how to use all the jets and showerheads. Water jets they give you, but no rubber bath mats."

"They probably would clash with the overall effect," Elizabeth said quietly, the memory of the luxury bathrooms still in her mind. "Did you break anything?"

"No, the shower is still in one piece," Richard said, a bit of his humor finally coming through. "Look, Elizabeth, we've canceled the remainder of my appearances, and all I want to do is get home and get my doctor to order the damn MRI that was suggested, to make sure I didn't do more than what the emergency room people said I did."

"Which is…?" Elizabeth asked, aware that Richard had said *damn* twice. He must really be in pain.

"Pulled muscles in my back and some mild contusions—in other words, I somehow managed to skin my damn knee on the shower drain when I went down. The only direct flight was in to Philly Airport, so I won't be back in Allentown until at least six. Can I count on you being at the house?"

"Yes, of course I'll be there. Where else would I be?" And then she winced, both at the thought of Will possibly taking them all to Dorney Park tomorrow afternoon that had raced into her head, and at the realization that she wasn't exactly jumping out of her skin with excitement at the thought of having Richard home. Then there was a third thought: How do I tell him I've decided my answer to his proposal is no…when the poor man is obviously in pain?

"Good. Thank you, Elizabeth. Ah, they're calling first class. If I start now, I can probably hobble onto the damn plane by Tuesday."

Elizabeth hit Off on the phone, ending the call Richard had already terminated, and sat back in the comfortably overstuffed chair. Well, now, hadn't reality sneaked up on her, just when she was beginning to like feeling like a girl again, like a woman again.

But she was a woman. A woman with two kids, a job and plenty of responsibility. Still, it had been fun while it lasted, even if it hadn't lasted quite a full twenty-four hours.

As Richard and his strong dose of muscle relaxants would say: *damn*.

Richard Halstead the writer was urbane, endlessly interesting, sometimes too absorbed in his work, but wonderfully intelligent.

Richard Halstead the man was kind, generous, polite and prone to avoid social engagements in favor of a round of golf or a snifter of brandy, a comfortable chair and the company of a good book.

Richard Halstead the patient could be taken out into the gardens and shot, and no jury would convict her.

He would move a little wrong in his chair and his yelp of pain would have her running to his side, sure he'd just popped a rib or something. At least for the first half-dozen times. After that, she just said, "Then don't move that way if you know it hurts when you move that way."

And he seemed to have this built-in radar that told him when she'd sat down to drink a cup of coffee, or had stolen a moment to phone over to the apartment to see if the twins were all right, and even when she'd opened the door to the bathroom, hoping for a few moments of privacy.

Because the moment she thought she finally had a free moment to herself was when she'd hear, "Elizabeth!"

"Elizabeth, I hate to ask, but could you possibly

make me a can of chicken noodle soup? With crackers?"

"Elizabeth, can you find my other reading glasses? These pinch at the nosepiece. And there's a book in my office I'd like to have. I can't remember the title, but it has a blue cover. Something on criminology. Or was that forensics? It's blue. I do know that."

"Elizabeth! I dropped the remote again. Could you come in here and pick it up for me? If you can't come right now I'll do it my— *Ow*, dammit!"

"He's worse than the twins. I should tie the thing around his neck with a big blue bow. That's what I should do," Elizabeth muttered as she walked through the foyer to answer the bell. It might be Sunday, but the doorbell had been ringing all morning with Get Well deliveries from Richard's agent, his publisher, his publicists and even from the radio station in Boulder he was supposed to be interviewing with at that very moment. John, his agent, had sent flowers and a bottle of aged brandy—how he'd managed that on a Sunday morning was anybody's guess. Elizabeth was beginning to consider cracking the thing open and chugging from the lovely brown bottle.

She pulled open the door, prepared to see another delivery person bending his head around an oversize vase of expensive hothouse flowers.

"Oh," she said, stepping back a pace. "Will. It's you."

Suddenly, for as uninhibited as he'd made her feel, as she'd gloried in feeling only two nights ago, she now felt as if she should cross her arms over her breasts or something in belated modesty.

"I've shown up at a bad time?" he asked, stepping into the foyer. "I did something stupid yesterday, Elizabeth. I suggested to Dan that we all go to Dorney Park today. I shouldn't have done that without clearing it with you. I realized that almost immediately. But now I don't want to let them down. Mike told me you were over here. I thought you said you were on vacation until your boss got back."

Elizabeth heard only about every third word as she stared at Will, realizing only belatedly that her mouth was open, and quickly shutting it. She'd had herself convinced. She was fine with what she'd told herself. Casual sex with a handsome man who was also a fabulous lover, no strings attached, no expectations. Everybody does it. Where's the harm?

He was so good with the twins. He had the nicest smile. He was just enough boy and just enough man. He was funny. And kind.

She should have known. She should have known she wasn't the sort of person who could have one-night stands, indiscriminate sex. Until Will came along, her only experience had been with Jamie, and that hadn't bothered her because making love was just that. The word was right there: *love*.

Oh, God...

"Elizabeth? You're angry that I talked to the boys about Dorney Park?"

She blinked, trying to drag her mind away from the startling revelation that had just smacked her in the chops. She was in love with Will Hollingswood.

"No, no, of course not. Won't you come—well, you already are in, aren't you?" Then she winced, her mind working in ways it shouldn't, a way it wouldn't have a week earlier.

"I should go out again? Your boss doesn't like strangers in his house when he's not home?"

"Elizabeth! I dropped the damn remote again!"

Will cocked one eyebrow as he looked at her. "I thought he was on some book tour or something."

"He was, until he took a fall and did something to his back. He arrived here this morning."

"And that means you're no longer on vacation," Will said, nodding. "It also means I promised the boys Dorney Park, and now they're going to be disappointed."

"I suppose so, yes." Elizabeth looked down the hall toward the family room, where Richard was undoubtedly trying to reach the remote that had slid off the arm of his leather chair yet again. "They have the entire summer ahead of them. They'll get there. I mean, not that you have to take them, because I certainly didn't mean that. I mean, that I can take them sometime. You shouldn't feel obligated in any—"

"Give," Will said, stepping closer to her, putting his arms lightly on her shoulders.

"Excuse me? What do you mean—*give?*"

"I don't know. The word seemed to work wonders when the boys were arguing in the backseat the other day. So," he said, moving one hand beneath her chin, and tilting her face upward. "Give. Please?"

And then he kissed her.

It wasn't a passionate kiss. Nor was it a demanding kiss.

And yet her entire body seemed to flush in response.

"Good," he said, smiling at her moments later, still holding her chin in his hand. "I've been wanting to do that since I left here the other night. Just to check."

She was so bemused that it took her a moment to ask, "Check what?"

"I'd wondered if something this good was just a dream, that's all," he said, bending in to kiss her cheek, then continuing with these brief kisses as he moved toward her mouth. "Could we check again?"

"Elizabeth? The remote? Is someone at the door? Never mind, you're busy. I'll get it my— *Ow!* Damn!"

Richard's exclamation had been immediately preceded by the sound of a thump. Elizabeth and Will looked at each other and then ran toward the sound.

"Richard!" Elizabeth exclaimed, seeing him on all fours on the carpet. "You should have waited for me."

"Sorry. I think I'm stuck."

He managed to push himself back onto his haunches before Will took hold of his arm and carefully guided him back into the chair behind him.

"Thank you," Richard said, gingerly easing against the back of the chair. "I was trying to save you a trip, Elizabeth. I hate being useless. Hello, who are you?"

Elizabeth quickly made the introductions, explaining that Will had come to take the twins to Dorney Park and the waterslides. She refused to compare the two men, especially since poor Richard was currently at such a disadvantage.

"Hollingswood," Richard repeated after the two men had shaken hands. "You play golf?"

"I do. Not often enough, however, especially now, coaching the kids. You play at Saucon, don't you?"

"Most of the time, yes. You?"

"Lehigh Links, when I can. It's part of my condo community," Will said, pulling up a chair and sitting down just as if he was an invited guest. Men. It was all so much easier for them. Mention golf, mention baseball or football and, bam, instant camaraderie. "But we're not going to compare handicaps if yours is less than twelve."

Richard nodded. "Tough course. Not that Saucon Valley is a cakewalk. Sorry I fell out of the chair. Just when I think I'm good, a shot of pain takes my breath away and I go flopping like some damn fish. All muscle, they told me in Denver, and once the spasm releases I'll be fine. That moment can't come too soon, although the pain pills are interesting. Elizabeth? Don't let us keep you if you were doing something else. You're on vacation, remember?"

"I—but—" Elizabeth gestured vaguely with both hands, as if attempting to grasp something that simply wasn't there. And then she gave up. "I'll go check on the twins."

"Tell them I'm still taking them to Dorney Park, if that's all right with you," Will called after her. She turned to look at him in amazement, but he and Richard were already deep in conversation again. She heard the name Tiger Woods being mentioned and knew she'd lost both men for at least the next half hour.

She headed straight for the foyer and the front door, leaving behind her could-be fiancé and her Friday-night lover.

"You couldn't make this stuff up," she muttered to herself as she hurried down the brick walk and turned toward the garage apartment.

And then it got worse.

She stopped as a car pulled into the long driveway, gliding to a stop beside her, and she saw Eve D'Allesandro hop out of the car, waving to her.

"Oh, good, here you are. I was hesitating up at the top of the drive, not knowing if I should go to the house—what a house!—or if you lived somewhere else on the property. Hang on, I'll be right there."

Elizabeth watched as Eve opened the rear door of her compact car, reached in and then emerged with a plastic grocery bag filled with books.

Elizabeth gave herself a mental head slap. How could she have forgotten? She'd agreed yesterday that Eve could drop off her Jake LaRue collection, and she'd have Richard sign the books for her when he got back from his tour.

"I really can't thank you enough," Eve said, handing her the bag of hardbacks. She'd double-bagged them, and the weight needed that extra support. "I can't believe I never knew he lives here. All his bio on the back page says is that he lives *outside Philadelphia.* Well, hell, the whole world lives outside Philly one way or another, except for those who live inside it."

Then she turned her head as a van with the name of a flower shop pulled into the driveway and parked behind her car. "Flowers?" she asked, frowning, and then smiled. "Ah…from the guy who lights your fire, perhaps?"

No, he's inside swapping golf stories with my almost-fiancé, as a matter of fact, Elizabeth thought, feeling more frantic by the moment. She had a quick vision of Lucy and Ethel shoving chocolates into their mouths, their chef's hats, their aprons, because too many chocolate candies were advancing toward them too quickly on the conveyor belt.

Elizabeth had people advancing toward her too fast on her personal conveyor belt. People and complications, all coming straight for her. If anyone had asked her a week ago, she would have said her life was all right but probably a little boring. Not anymore!

And, it soon became obvious, a fruit basket the size of a small country was the next thing coming down that conveyor belt toward her.

"Back again the same day," the deliveryman said, peeking out from behind the mountain of produce and bright yellow cellophane. "Hope Mr. Halstead is better soon, although the overtime pay isn't so bad. You want me to carry this into the house? It's pretty heavy."

Elizabeth clasped her hands together, looking from the delivery guy to Eve to the house, and then she smiled in resignation and waved a hand in the direction of the brick path. "Sounds like a plan. Eve, would you like to meet Richard?"

"Does a bear— Good God, woman, you mean he's *here?*" Eve whipped a small hand mirror out of her oversize purse and examined her reflection. "Okay, once out of direct sunlight, I shouldn't look too bad. Let's do it!"

Once the fruit was on the kitchen island, the delivery guy tipped generously a second time and on his way back to his truck, Elizabeth joined Eve in the foyer once more. "Chessie's cousin Will is in with him now," she told Eve, figuring she might as well get her lies in early if not often. "He's the twins' baseball coach, and he's taking them to Dorney Park to go on the water-slides."

"Why would he do that?" Eve asked, frowning. "I mean, I *know* Will Hollingswood, and he's not the take a-bunch-of-kids-to-a-water-park kind of guy. Unless there's a topless beach there nobody told me about— just kidding! And, hey, are you sure this is all right? I mean, me barging in on your boss like this? What with him sick and all?"

"Not sick. He had a fall and wrenched his back. It's supposedly some sort of muscle spasm. That's why he's not on his tour. He got home from Colorado early this morning. It'll be fine. You'll cheer him up. He loves meeting fans."

Elizabeth didn't realize what an understatement her assurances were until they'd walked into the family room and she'd introduced Eve to Richard.

The man nearly killed himself trying to get to his feet to welcome her, and when he winced in pain, it was Eve who reacted first, quickly grabbing on to him and helping to ease him back into his chair.

"Looks like you really did a number on yourself, huh?" Eve said, sitting down in the chair Will had just vacated and eyeing him speculatively. "You know, in my long and varied career, I was once a certified massage therapist. Really. I still keep my license current, although I don't know why. I'm betting that's all you really need—a good massage, followed by a nice hot shower with the water pounding down on those sore muscles."

"It was a shower that got me into this mess," Richard told her, but he was smiling. "What's in the bag?"

Elizabeth had put the bag down on the floor beside Eve and backed away from it as she would a wicker basket that might just hold a cobra. Richard had been restrained, yet somewhat testy, all morning long. She wasn't sure this was the time to ask him to whip out the old pen and autograph a dozen books, making sure he wrote something different and witty in each one.

"Oh, those?" Eve said, gesturing toward the bag. "Now you'll make me blush, because I didn't know you were here and Elizabeth said she'd feed them to you one at a time so you wouldn't feel too bothered by a drooling fan. That would be me. It's all of your books," she ended, as if realizing she hadn't quite made that part clear. "Dog-eared and read at least three times each. I think Jake LaRue must be the sexiest man alive. I'm so ashamed."

She didn't look ashamed. She looked…dazzling.

And Richard? Richard looked…dazzled.

Elizabeth looked at Will, who was grinning at her in a way that made her—and she was by and large a well-tempered person—want to smack him in the chops. He sidled up close to her and said quietly, "Do you think we should leave these two alone and sneak off to the water park? I did pretty much promise the boys. Besides, I've been dying to see you in a bathing suit anyway."

She didn't remind him that he'd seen her naked. She was trying hard not to remind herself of that fact.

"Richard needs someone to stay with him, and Elsie is due at her mother's for early dinner. She goes to early dinner at her mother's every Sunday. I've already got a rump roast in the oven. So we can't go."

Eve, who it would seem possessed the keen hearing of a bat, looked up at Elizabeth, her gaze shifting rather knowingly toward Will for a heartbeat before she smiled helpfully. "I have nothing going on today. If you two have promised the boys something, you really shouldn't renege without a good reason. I'm still rather upset with my mother for not following through on that pony she promised me. Granted, I think she'd said it just to shut me up, but I really was counting on that pony. And I think I know what to do with a rump roast, so Richard here won't starve."

"You like horses, Eve?" Richard asked her. "I haven't ridden in years, why, I really don't know, but it used to be a passion of mine. Would you care for something to drink?"

"Well, I'd love a scotch, to celebrate meeting my favorite author, but it's a little early for that, and I have to drive home. How about a diet soda?"

"I'll get—" Elizabeth began, but Richard was already halfway out of his chair. A flash of pain crossed his face, but he seemed to tamp it down, exchanging it for a smile as Eve hopped to her feet to help support him.

"Very good," Eve complimented him. "But I can show you a trick on how to stand up and sit back down again without hurting yourself. It's all in the correct use of your upper body. Ah, and from the feel of that bicep, you've got plenty of upper-body strength." The two of them headed for the kitchen, Eve still with her arm slipped through Richard's elbow. She turned her head to wink at Elizabeth. "You just go, hon. I'll hold down the fort here."

Then she turned her attention back to Richard, who seemed to be walking a lot better than he had when he'd first come in the door from the airport. "Two-to-one odds I can work that knot out of your back, Richard. I'll just get you flat on your bed, and that knot will be gone in no time. Wanna give it a try?"

"If you're willing, sure. Thank you, Eve."

Elizabeth just stood where she was, her mouth open, slowly shaking her head. Who was that masked man who'd just gone off with Eve as if she'd asked him if he wanted "a lollipop, little boy?"

"Well, that's all settled," Will said, standing close behind her. When had he moved? "Nice guy. Do you think it's fair, siccing Eve on him?"

"He, um, he didn't seem to mind," Elizabeth said, turning around to face Will. "Still, I don't know if I can leave him. He is my employer."

"And it is Sunday," Will reminded her. "He said you should go. Besides, I promised the boys. I know, I know, I shouldn't have done that, but I don't like breaking promises. Breaking promises to kids just makes it worse."

She sighed, nodding her head. "They've been talking about Dorney Park nonstop since you were here yesterday. And I'm not being gracious, which I should be, because volunteering to watch the twins run berserk in a park filled with wave pools and waterslides is a sacrifice above and beyond the call of duty."

Will grinned. "You just proved why you have to go with us, the lawyer in me feels it necessary to point out, Ms. Carstairs. The defense rests."

"Good for you, Counselor," Elizabeth muttered, trying not to smile as they headed for the front door. "Because it's probably the *only* rest you're going to get for the next five or six hours."

Chapter Nine

Will sat on the bench beside the walkway leading to the carousel and watched as Elizabeth, just leaving a small refreshment stand across the way, prudently wrapped napkins around the paper cups holding scoops of rainbow water ice before handing them back to Mike and Dan.

After three hours of enjoying the water park as seen through the eyes of a pair of seven-year-olds, Will was now enjoying the sight of a beautiful, enticing, oblivious-to-her-charms mother of two who, apparently, had been using him to decide if she wanted to marry the very nice, personable, wealthy and rock-solid bestselling author, Richard Halstead. Not that Chessie had said that, exactly. No, that part had been his cousin's bright idea.

Then again, a reasonable person or, at the least, a defense attorney, might point out that he was here only because his cousin had blackmailed him into being nice to a lonely young widow. No. Wrong, Counselor. That was last week. He was here *now* because Elizabeth Carstairs was the most fascinating creature he'd ever met, and he could hardly believe his luck at having found her, found her two wonderful sons, found a new meaning in a life he'd thought was perfect until real perfection had actually entered it and smacked him in the face.

And if Elizabeth knew he'd initially gone after her because of some twisted, half-baked plan of Chessie's, she'd shove one of those water ices in his face and refuse to ever see him again.

Elizabeth and the boys were distracted by one of the park employees dressed up in a huge, fuzzy cartoon-character suit that had to make the warm, sunny day feel like he was working in the second level of hell.

The twins were laughing at the cartoon animal's antics, joining in with other young children who were vying for the character's attention.

Will took the opportunity to look at Elizabeth. Of all the sights at the amusement park—and there were many—none interested him so much as the vision of youth and happiness she so effortlessly exuded with her unconscious grace and delighted smile.

Her still-damp hair pulled back into a casual ponytail, her nose shiny from the chlorine and a touch of sun she'd picked up at the water park, she looked young, carefree, and still as sexually appealing to him as she had in his bed, with moonlight streaming across the sheets, caressing her enticing curves as he traced his hand over her bare hip.

Will had been a firm believer in the idea that a woman, once a mother, was no longer—oh God, what an admission!—really a woman. That she was a mother first, a wife second or third and a woman last of all.

When he was wrong, he could be more wrong than anyone he knew.

Marriage was something years in the future, for when he got tired of late nights and endless women who were both forgettable and interchangeable. Children? He hadn't even considered children in his life.

Now he was considering both.

This wasn't him. He was selfish. He was self-centered. He did nothing unless it was his idea, pleased him, benefited him in some way. Dorney Park? He hadn't been to Dorney Park since he was a kid, and they'd only had one wooden roller coaster, not this dazzling array of coasters and dancing cartoon characters and wave pools. He'd outgrown that sort of entertainment, much preferring a trip to Philadelphia or New York to see a show. When he was in the water, that water was clear blue, tropical and bordered white sandy beaches.

Maybe he'd been in the sun too long. Maybe that foul ball at practice the other day had hit his head a little harder than he'd thought at the time.

Maybe he should drop the baseball team, take the jail

time and the doubled fine, and save himself before it was too late….

The cartoon character with the fuzzy head the size of a large Pilates exercise ball grabbed the twins' hands and began dancing with them to the song playing over the park's sound system.

Will recognized the song, an oldie-but-goodie from the Beach Boys in their heyday.

Elizabeth was standing at the edge of the small crowd, laughing and clapping her hands in time to the music as she watched the boys try to mimic the steps of their new friend.

Suddenly, before he could let sanity into his brain, Will got to his feet and walked over to her, slipping his arm around her waist. "Let's show them how it's done," he said, grabbing her left hand and stepping into what he hoped was the jitterbug.

She followed him as if they'd been dancing together forever.

Parents clapped. Children goggled. Mike and Dan shouted encouragement.

There was nothing tentative about Elizabeth's response. She didn't seem to care that they were in an amusement park, that she was a *mom* or that he was the man who had only recently taken her to his bed and had made no promises once that incredible, wildly passionate interlude was over.

She was intelligent, beautiful; she loved life. Her ponytail swung back and forth as they broke apart, as they came together again, as he twirled her under his arm, as he danced them in circles to the beat of silly bubblegum music. Her unaffected smile and shining bright eyes sent a sucker punch to his gut.

And Will knew he was in big, big trouble....

They sat shoulder-to-shoulder on the bottom step of the wooden slat stairs that led up to her apartment over the garages. It was more dark than dusk, and both boys had been asleep almost before their heads hit the pillows. Mikey, in fact, had nearly nodded off while brushing his teeth at the bathroom sink.

Elizabeth folded her hands and rested them on her knees, looking out on the vast grounds of Richard's estate at the fireflies that had just begun blinking as they circled the area as if performing their nightly rounds.

"It's beautiful here, isn't it?"

She could feel Will's eyes on her as he answered. "It's beautiful anywhere you are," he said, and then laughed self-deprecatingly. "And that was one of the worst lines I've ever uttered. As a defense lawyer, I've uttered more than my share. But I mean it, Elizabeth. You're a beautiful woman, inside and out."

Elizabeth lowered her chin, wishing she could be flattered but knowing that she was a fraud. Will was becoming more interested in her. She wasn't an oblivious teenager; she knew he was interested. She was worried at her own reaction to him, feeling as if everything was happening too quickly, that she might have thought she was taking baby steps back into life, but suddenly she'd found herself poised at the edge of a cliff.

The next step, if she took it, was going to be a doozy.

"I should go see how Richard is feeling. We've been gone a long time."

"I wouldn't do that. Eve's car is still in the other driveway. I've known Eve for a long time, and *shy* and *retiring* aren't words I'd use to describe her. Do you really want to drop in unannounced?"

Elizabeth turned to him, her eyes wide in shock. "You…you think that— Oh, don't be ridiculous. Richard isn't like that."

"Really? How do you know?"

"I know because—" She stopped, closed her mouth before she said *because he's never been like that with me.* "Because," she said desperately, "he couldn't even bend over to pick up the remote control earlier today."

Will leaned in, kissed her cheek. "Beautiful *and* innocent. Let me put it this way. When we left, Eve, trained massage therapist and admitted fan-girl of the great man, was talking about getting him into bed, stripping him to his waist—at least that far—and then oiling up her hands and rubbing them all over him. And I didn't hear Richard objecting, did you? The mental picture I get is of Eve, skirt hiked up, straddling your injured boss across his thighs as she really leans into the massage, all while telling him how handsome and talented he is. That's a lot of…muscle stimulus going on, Elizabeth."

Her face was burning. She knew it was. "I…I've never seen—that is, I've never *pictured* Richard as being that way. I mean, I've read his books. I know that Jake LaRue is rather, um, is rather *active* with the—but you don't have to kill somebody to write about murder, do you?"

"Some research is more fun than other kinds, I imagine," Will said, his voice still teasing, his smile visible in the now rapidly fading light.

Elizabeth looked toward the house. For the first time she noticed that there were no lights on downstairs, but only a faint bit of light visible around the corner windows of Richard's bedroom suite.

"Well, that's going to make it easier," she said before she could clap a hand over her traitorous mouth.

"Pardon me? I think you've lost me. What makes what easier?"

"Hmm?" Elizabeth was slipping into her own private thoughts, at least one of them making her quite ashamed of herself. "Um…easier that I don't have to go back over to the house tonight, that's all." She reached into her pocket and pulled out the small receiver for the baby monitor she carried with her when she had to leave the boys alone to do something for Richard. "I know this thing works, but I still don't like leaving them, even though they're asleep and I'm only about one hundred yards away."

Will put his hand beneath her chin. "You're embarrassed. I made you see Richard as someone other than your boss, as a man, and I've embarrassed you."

"I suppose so," she said, getting to her feet and stepping onto the grass, putting some distance between them. "Richard is more than my boss, though."

And then she stopped. They'd had such a wonderful, even memorable, day. She didn't want to end it by telling Will how she'd so blatantly used him. *Dear God, he thought he was taking me to bed while I was taking him to bed. What kind of person am I?*

"Do you suppose it will be back to work for you both tomorrow morning?"

"I suppose so. I was just beginning to enjoy the idea of having a week's vacation when he called to say he was coming home. Now he's here, and I don't know what I should be doing."

Will stood up, as well. "You could ask him to hang a sock over the front door knob if he's tied up," he suggested, still with that infuriating grin on his face. "Can we take a walk? You said that thing works all the way to Richard's house, so it has to work the same distance in the other direction."

Elizabeth almost involuntarily looked up the length of the stairs, not knowing if she was doing a "mental eye check" on her sons or considering making a break for it. "Sure," she said, knowing how silly she was being. "It is a nice night."

He slipped his arm around her shoulders as they began leisurely walking across the lawn toward the tennis court, where a vapor light turned an area of the court a soft white-blue. Crickets chirped in the undergrowth, and lightning bugs lit their little yellow lamps here and there, like stars blinking near the grass.

"I suppose the boys will want to catch them again, as they're fascinated by the glow," she said, pointing in the general direction of the lightning bugs. "They always let them go again the next morning. I thought I'd have trouble getting them to do that at first, so I started telling them all that business about if you love something let it go—but by then the lid was already off the jar and the boys were running for their bikes. It turns out that lightning bugs are not half as interesting when they're not putting on a show. In the morning they're just bugs."

"That's very profound, in a disturbing sort of way, considering that I'm put in mind of our last time together," Will said, stopping on the grass and turning her so that he could rest his hands on her shoulders. "I hope you don't think that I'm only interested in you when you're...glowing."

He'd surprised her. "I didn't mean it that way at all."

"No, of course you didn't. That was probably my guilty conscience twisting the meaning. Do you know you're not my type, Elizabeth?"

"If you mean, do I remember Kay Quinlan, yes, I've considered that."

"Ah, yes, Kay. She was never important to me, or I to her, now that I think about it. No woman has ever been important to me. That makes me pretty much a bastard, doesn't it?"

"I don't think there's a Boy Scout merit badge for fooling around, no," she said, becoming more and more uncomfortable by the moment. She didn't know real people had conversations like this. She'd certainly never imagined herself a part of one of them, that much was certain.

Will shook his head slightly. "You're not as sweet and innocent as you look, are you? You know what I'm saying. But do you know what I mean? What I'm not saying? Because for a man who gets his kicks making fantastic pitches to juries, I'm doing a really lousy job of defending myself."

"Maybe that's because your client isn't innocent," Elizabeth said quietly. "Then again, Will, no one is. Totally innocent, I mean. We all do things we're sorry for, even when our intentions had seemed reasonable at the time. I know I have, even very recently."

"Do you want to talk about it?"

What was he doing? Did he want her to confess to something so that he could confess to something and then they could both tell each other to forget it, it's all right and then move on?

And move on to what?

"No, I don't think so," she said, and she would have backed up, except that he had now slid his hands down her sides to cup her waist, hold her where she was.

"I don't, either. Sometimes what we think is important isn't really all that earthshattering, or at least it's something better left unsaid, something that could only hurt something good."

"Will?" Elizabeth cocked her head to one side. "I think you're scaring me. You have something to tell me, don't you?"

"I might. And you might have something to tell me?"

"I might." She took a deep breath, let it out on a sigh. "Sometime."

"But not tonight?"

She shook her head. "I don't think so, no. There's somebody else who has to hear it first."

"But we're good?" Will asked her, pulling her closer.

"I didn't know we were bad," she said, raising a hand to stroke his cheek.

"We're not. But we could be. How soundproof are the walls in that apartment anyway?"

Excitement replaced nervousness instantly. "It's a very old building. The walls are quite thick. I know, because the guy from the telephone company taught the boys a few new words when he was trying to run cable through the interior walls. But...I've never...I've never had a man in the house, Will. We'd have to be very quiet."

He was touching her, running his fingertips lightly up and down her sides, turning her knees to water. "I can't be held responsible for what *you* might do," he said teasingly. "Although it could be interesting, searching for the limits of your self-control."

"Is that a challenge? We see who *breaks* first? Who makes the first sound?" Elizabeth thought she might fall down where she was. She hadn't experienced verbal foreplay until this point in her life. Man, the things you didn't realize you'd missed...

He was nuzzling at her temple now, his breaths rather shallow and quick as he whispered, "I want you so much I ache with the wanting." As if to prove his words, he slipped his thigh between hers and pulled her closer, so that she readily felt the evidence of his arousal. "I've never wanted anyone so much in my life."

By now he was pressing kisses against the side of her neck, and she tilted her head to give him greater access, biting her bottom lip between her teeth as her body rocked with each new sensation. She wanted. She wanted so much.

All day, the tension between them had been building. She knew it. She'd known he'd felt it, as well.

She boldly slid her hand between their bodies, turning it so that her palm pressed against his arousal, so that she could cup him, feel the strong maleness of him through the material of his slacks. A lightning bolt of desire flashed white-hot through her as he softly moaned his pleasure, encouraging her. "Do…do we have to go upstairs? The bed is so far away…"

She'd already known that he'd need little encouragement, and the next thing she knew he had lifted her in his arms and was carrying her toward the gazebo just to the left of the tennis court.

Elizabeth was Rapunzel, released at last from her lonely tower. She was the rescued princess being carried off atop the white knight's trusty steed. She was every fairy tale taken to its most romantic conclusion, every fantasy ever written or dreamed.

The thick cushions of the chaise lounge welcomed them to their private bower. The soft breeze wafted the intoxicating scent of climbing roses to them but was not able to cool their heated skin as their clothing was discarded, as their mouths clung, their hands raced over each soft curve, each firm, rippling muscle.

"I feel…I feel so decadent."

"You taste so good…."

"Oh, yes, please…do that."

"All day…I've thought of nothing but this all day… all of my life…"

"I didn't know…I never knew there could be…this."

"Pleasing you…it's all I want."

"No, no…you, too. I want you inside of me…as deep as you can be." Elizabeth raked her fingernails over his bare back, drawing him to her even as she raised her hips to him, needing to be filled, demanding to be filled with the heat of him.

"Elizabeth!" he cried out, plunging into her, captured there as she scissored her long legs around his back.

Her jaw was tight with need, her muscles straining with the intensity of the arousal he'd brought her to with his mouth, his tongue, his wonderfully exploring fingers.

"Yes, yes," she encouraged, her need for him removing any inhibitions. "Deeper, Will. Harder, faster…"

And then she felt it, that special, white-hot melting of every part of her, the complete loss of everything in the world except this man, this moment.

He must have sensed her total surrender to his body. He went faster, deeper, harder, his own storm building, raging out of control.

Elizabeth's body clenched and unclenched around his, ecstasy building with each carnal sensation. But it was when she felt Will's release that she flew beyond mere carnal pleasure and into the realm of the magnificent.

They were no longer two. They were one. One perfect whole.

When, finally spent, he collapsed onto her, Elizabeth reveled in his weight, the triumph of having pleased him. She stroked his damp back, pressed kisses against his cheek and ear, smiled as his breath came short and fast, as if he'd just run a long race.

"You…you're unbelievable," Will said at last, rolling onto his side and propping himself so that he could look down into her face. He ran his fingertips down her cheek. "I didn't hurt you?"

"No," she said, smiling, and then turning her mouth so that she could press a kiss into his palm. "You could never hurt me. I wouldn't be here if I believed that you could."

He didn't answer her, and the light from the tennis court showed her that his eyes had lost some of their animation.

"Will?"

He kissed her, and then sat up on the edge of the chaise lounge, reaching for his clothing.

She sat up, pressed her cheek against his back. "Will? What did I say?"

"Nothing, sweetheart," he assured her, but his tone was flat. "How about we get dressed and finish that walk we were going to take?"

"And start that talk we were going to have?" she asked him, looking toward the house, and the dim light showing around the edges of Richard's bedroom windows. "Yes, maybe we should."

KASEY MICHAELS
181

Will stood up, zipping his slacks, and looked down at her, making her feel self-conscious that she was just then hooking her bra. Maybe she wasn't as blasé and modern as she thought.

"But we're going to remember this—what just happened here, what we're discovering about each other— when we have that talk. Promise me, Elizabeth. It's not where we start but where we end up that matters."

Elizabeth felt a chill skitter down her spine as she pulled her sleeveless tank over her head, momentarily hiding her face from him. Did he already know? Had Chessie told him? God, he must feel like some sort of a guinea pig she was using for her experiment—whatever that experiment had been.

"Will, I didn't plan—"

The baby monitor that had been abandoned on the floor of the gazebo crackled into life. "Mom! Mom! Mikey's sick! Oh, gross, it's everywhere! MOM!"

Elizabeth didn't know how she managed to slip her feet into her shoes. But suddenly she was on her feet, and Will had hold of her hand, and they were racing down the few steps from the gazebo and running across the grass toward the garage apartment.

She was a terrible mother. Alone! She'd left her boys alone. She should have been there, she would have heard Mikey stir, been there when he got sick. She'd let them both eat too much junk food today. The water, the rides, all that sun—it was all just too much. My baby. *My poor, poor baby. Mommy's so sorry!*

Will stepped aside to allow her to run up the stairs

ahead of him but was right behind her when she skidded into the twins' room and flipped on the overhead light.

Danny was sitting cross-legged in the middle of his bed, wide-eyed as he hugged his favorite stuffed animal, watching Mikey, who was curled up in a small ball in the other bed.

"Mikey, honey, what's wrong?" Elizabeth said, carefully stepping around the evidence of her son's stomach upset and sitting down on the edge of the bed. "It's all right. We'll clean this up. Do you feel better now?"

Mikey shook his head, his eyes—his father's eyes—looking up at her in mute appeal. "My belly hurts."

"Still? Mikey, do you think you're going to throw up again?"

Once more the negative shake of the child's head. "It just hurts." He had his arms crossed low on his belly. "Ow! Ow, ow, ow! Mommy, make it stop."

"Do you think it was something he ate at the park?" Will asked from behind her.

Elizabeth turned her head to see that Will was holding Danny, who was clinging to him, his arms and legs wrapped around him, his head buried against Will's chest. Seeking comfort, reassurance.

Her heart nearly broke.

"I don't think so. He should have felt at least marginally better for a few minutes after he was sick. Before he was sick again, I mean. Mikey? Show Mommy where it hurts, okay?"

"He-here," Mikey said, reluctantly moving his arms, and then pressing his hand just below his navel before grabbing on to himself again, turning onto his side. "It hurts all the time. It really, really hurts."

"Okay, honey," Elizabeth soothed as she reached over to stroke his sweat-soaked curls. She looked to Will. "He's really hot," she said. "Maybe it's some sort of virus?"

"But you don't think so," Will said, adjusting the clinging Danny in his arms. "It's been a lot of years since I've watched my own mother in action, but I recognize that tone and that look on your face. Your mother's intuition is kicking in, isn't it?"

"I'm probably wrong," Elizabeth admitted, getting to her feet. "I need to think horses, not zebras."

"Okay, now you've lost me."

"Don't look for the exotic," she said, her eyes once more on Mikey, who rarely complained when he bumped his head or skinned his knee. Unlike Danny, who seemed to need a bandage for every imagined boo-boo. "But ever since Jamie, I—I'm probably overreacting."

"And what if you're not? I've got nothing else to do. You want him checked, then we get him checked."

Mikey leaned over the edge of the mattress and retched a single time before falling back against his pillow, his face nearly as white as the pillowcase. And then he started to cry. Really hard. Mikey wasn't a crier.

"You don't mind? I could call his pediatrician, but he'd probably just tell me to take him in if I thought he needed to go," she said as she got to her feet, opening Mikey's chest of drawers and pulling out a clean pair of pajamas.

To answer her, Will hefted Danny higher against his chest. "Okay, Dan the Man, how about we go get you strapped into your booster seat while Mom gets Mike dressed. You have slippers?"

Elizabeth was ahead of him, having grabbed Danny's slippers from under his bed, and slipped them on his feet. "We'll be right there."

But by the time Elizabeth had washed Mikey's hands and face and gotten him dressed in the clean pajamas, Will was back.

"Mike? Hey, Mike, here's the deal. I'm going to lift you, and you're going to tell me if I hurt you. But I'm going to be really, really careful, because I know you're hurting. We have a deal?"

Mikey, his eyes wide with pain, bit his bottom lip and nodded.

Elizabeth followed them, grabbing her purse from the kitchen table because she'd need her health insurance cards, and within ten minutes of hearing Danny's voice over the baby monitor, they were all in her car and on their way to the Emergency Room.

Will drove, without asking her, and she was grateful, sure she was shaking too hard not to run the SUV into a ditch. Instead, she sat in the backseat, wedged between the two booster seats. Danny clutched her one hand, Mikey the other.

It had been that way for such a long time. She and her boys against the large, indifferent world.

But tonight she could see the back of Will's head as he drove competently, only five miles over the speed limit, assuring the twins, assuring her, that everything was going to be all right. Everything was going to be just fine.

Tears pricked at Elizabeth's eyes, and she blinked them away, not wanting the boys to see her cry.

This was what she had wanted. To not be alone anymore. To not have every decision be only in her hands. To feel safe. To feel secure. To make the world better for her boys.

She hadn't counted on feeling loved.

Will hadn't been inside a hospital Emergency Room since he'd taken a baseball to the head during his junior year in college.

It was both comforting and maddening to know that emergency rooms never changed.

"Are you open to bribes?" he asked the nurse in charge after they'd been handed a pink kidney-shaped plastic basin and told to have a seat in the waiting area. Mikey had used the pan twice, and he was still crying, still looking like one sick puppy.

"Sir, we're lining patients up in the hallways," the nurse told him, not for the first time. "Your son will be seen in order of the severity of his complaint."

"He's not—" Will shut his mouth, as he'd been about to deny that Mikey was his son. If he did that, would Nurse Ratched here let him through those damn doors, or would Elizabeth have to go it alone back there in the examination room? "Look, Nurse, I know I'm driving you nuts, but what if it's his appendix? What if it bursts while you're guarding that door like some—no, I'm sorry. I won't say it. Just get the kid back there, okay? How do you let a kid sit out here in pain like this?"

The nurse consulted the sheet of paper in front of her. "The name again?"

"Holl— Hallelujah, and thank you," Will improvised quickly. "It's Carstairs. Michael Carstairs. He's seven. And he's scared. His brother's scared. His mom is scared."

"And you're the epitome of calm," the nurse said, but she smiled. "I see here that Michael is next, Mr. Carstairs. Feel better now, or am I going to have to find a doctor to prescribe a sedative?"

"Everybody's a comedian," Will muttered under his breath as he headed back to the kiddie corner, where Dan was playing at some sort of weird activity table with colorful twisted wires holding impaled wooden beads he could move. Who invented this stuff?

He was just about to sit down next to Elizabeth, who was holding Mike in her lap, when a nurse called out "Carstairs." Will grabbed Mike, figuring they had to let him in if he was the one carrying the kid, for crying out loud, and Elizabeth followed with Dan.

"Sorry, no one under twelve except the patient," the nurse told them when they reached the double doors.

"Ah, come on, they're twins. Inseparable. And Dan will be good. Won't you, Dan?"

"Let the kid in, Mary," the nurse at the desk said, hooking a thumb at Will. "*He's* the one who'll give you trouble."

"Thank you," Will told the nurse, as if she'd just complimented him, and the "Carstairs family" all made it past the double doors and into an exam room.

"We're probably in for another wait. This is only the second plateau. It could be a while before we see the doctor. You don't have to stay," Elizabeth told him as she pulled off Mike's pajamas to get him ready to be examined. "And I probably overreacted. He seems a little better."

At which point Mike made use of the kidney-shaped pan yet again.

The next hour would always be a bit of a blur for Will. White coats. Too many questions, all of which Elizabeth answered with a rapidity and precision that amazed him. A large needle going into a skinny little arm while Will held Mikey's other hand and told the kid to watch as he made a face like a monkey, in order to distract him.

The wait for the blood-test results.

Saying goodbye to Mikey outside the operating room, holding on to Dan, who worriedly wanted to know if his brother was going to "die like my daddy did."

He could see Elizabeth almost physically take hold of her composure, her chin lifting as she told her son that it was just a little operation, just an appendix that wasn't behaving and had to go, and that Mikey might even be able to come home tomorrow.

And then they waited.

Danny crawled onto Will's lap and was almost immediately asleep. Will tried to get Elizabeth to sit down beside him, rest her head on his shoulder, but he might as well have asked her to hop the next plane to the Bahamas.

She paced the empty surgical waiting room, hugging herself, beating herself up.

"I should have seen something. There have to be signs, don't there? But he seemed fine when I put him to bed."

"He *was* fine, Elizabeth," Will assured her. "You heard the doctor. Sometimes these things fester for months, and sometimes they hit out of the blue. There was nothing to see when you put him to bed because he was fine when you put him to bed."

She was quiet for a few minutes as she continued to pace. "I hate hospitals. Jamie hated when he had to go to the hospital. There was never any good news."

Will only nodded, letting her speak. They had to talk about her dead husband at some point. If she needed to talk now, then he needed to listen.

"His kind of cancer moved very fast. One minute he was joking that we needed to make love more often, that he was sore from lack of use. And the next they were telling us it was stage-four testicular cancer."

She stopped pacing, turned to face Will. "How could that be? We couldn't understand, we couldn't take it in. We had two babies, not even three years old. God, Will, *we* were little more than babies ourselves." She sighed audibly as she looked around the sparsely decorated waiting room. "I'm sorry. Too many memories sneaking up on me…"

She whipped her head toward the hallway as a woman clad in blue scrubs appeared, asking for Mikey's mommy and daddy.

"I'm Elizabeth Carstairs, Mikey's mother. Is it over?"

"It is, and he did just fine. Nasty little appendix, though, but still in one piece and just waiting for me to snip it. We'll be moving Mikey to a room in Pediatrics in a little bit, but he's pretty sleepy. I suggest you get his brother home to bed and come back in the morning. Mikey should be discharged in the afternoon."

"But he's all right? It was definitely his appendix and nothing else? It didn't burst?"

Will stood up, adjusting the sleeping Dan in his arms. "That's what the doctor said, sweetheart. A horse, not a pony. But definitely not a zebra."

"No, not a zebra. Not this time. Thank God. May I see him, doctor? Just for a moment? I mean, I know he's sleeping, and it's important that Danny sees that I think Mikey's well enough that I can leave him for a few hours—but I'm really torn."

The doctor smiled. "I'll tell you what I tell all my parents struggling with the same situation. We're here, we'll watch Mikey for you, and call you the moment he wakes up and asks for you. In the meantime," she said, waving a hand toward Danny, "you've got a sleepy little guy there who probably is more scared than he's letting on. He needs you, too."

Elizabeth swiped quickly at her eyes, wiping away tears. "Thank you. May I see Mikey now?"

Twenty minutes later they were on their way back to

Saucon Valley, with Dan asleep in his booster seat and Elizabeth now in the front seat beside Will, but very quiet.

He carried Dan down the hall while Elizabeth mumbled something about making them both glasses of iced tea. He laid the child in Elizabeth's bed, as she still had some cleaning up to do in the twins' bedroom, and realized it seemed like years since he'd been imagining himself lying in that bed beside her.

He bent over the sleeping boy and kissed his forehead, already missing the weight of Dan's body against his, the trust that had been put in him. It was the most terrible, awe-inspiring feeling in the world. To be responsible for a child. It was both the most frightening and the best feeling a man could ever be blessed enough to have in his lifetime.

He returned to the kitchen to see Elizabeth standing at the countertop, two empty glasses in front of her, a chilled pitcher of iced tea next to them. She wasn't moving, except for the rather tortured rise and fall of her shoulders as she breathed in and out.

She'd been a brick. She'd made all the right decisions. She'd done what had to be done, and she'd done it splendidly.

Will walked up behind her, touched his hands to her shoulders, turning her around so that he could pull her into his arms. "Give," he said quietly, pressing a kiss against her hair. "Let it go, sweetheart. You're not alone. I'm not going to let you be alone. You don't always have to be strong. Just let it go."

He held her, his heart aching for her, and let her cry.

Chapter Ten

Mikey was not a happy camper. He got to go to base-ball practice every day, but he wasn't allowed to play. He was relegated to sitting in a chair on the hill and watching his brother, Danny, run around on the field.

Elizabeth got to play referee when Mikey teased Danny about a dropped ball and when Danny shot back that at least he could *play* while Mikey had to sit on the hill like a *girl.*

Ah, brotherly love. There was nothing like it.

And she, sitting on the hill beside Mikey, catering to his every need at home, had been relegated to watching Will from that same hill, or watching him with the boys when he stopped at the apartment, usually a man bearing gifts. He seemed to know that she wasn't ready for anything else from him, not right now.

Mikey's emergency had brought back memories of those horrible last months with Jamie, and she'd needed to work through them, finally come to terms with both her loss and the fact that life, because she had her boys, needed to move on. She needed to move on.

Will seemed to understand this without her saying a word. He gave her space while at the same time letting her know he was there for her.

Mostly, the twins took her full attention, when she wasn't over at the house, trying to get Richard to stop avoiding her.

He'd told her to still consider herself on vacation and to go take care of her patient. He was fine on his own. His back was better, as if the fall had never happened. In fact, he was going to play golf on Friday. In the meantime, he'd just putter around his office, see if he could get his mind back into his latest Jake LaRue manuscript.

Elizabeth pretended not to notice that Richard's car was gone every evening and that sometimes it wasn't back at the house until midmorning of the next day.

Richard didn't talk about it.

She didn't talk about it.

It was getting very *loud,* neither of them talking about it.

At the same time, she and Will weren't talking about anything, either. It wasn't just that he was giving her space to come to terms with her emotions. Danny's yell for help had interrupted her just as she'd been about to confess what she'd done, and it might only be a suspicion, but she was pretty sure that Will had been equally glad to have a reprieve.

What did he have to tell her? She knew he had something on his mind, but except to think that he knew about Richard, what could be bothering him? Had he been about to say that fun was fun, her kids were great, he really liked having sex with her, but he felt it might be time he moved on?

No, she wasn't in any hurry to either confess to Will or hear him confess to her.

Besides, first she had to talk to Richard.

"Have a minute?" Elizabeth asked, poking her head into his office on Thursday morning, part of her wanting to postpone what she had to say, the rest of her just wishing she could get it over with and both of them could stop pretending. Of course, Richard didn't know that she was pretending, did he? He might even think he was breaking her heart, or at least her hopes for a secure financial future for the twins. What a mess!

"Could we talk later, Elizabeth? I'm on sort of a roll here." He continued typing, not looking up from the keyboard.

"It is rather important."

Richard frowned at the computer screen, and then waved her into the room. She couldn't help but notice that he'd activated the screen saver. She knew what that meant—the man was writing a love scene. Or, as he called Jake LaRue's exploits, a *sex* scene. Only women make love, Richard had informed her. Men have sex.

"How's the boy? Danny, correct?"

"Mikey," Elizabeth said, smiling ruefully. "But you were close."

"Well, I did have a fifty-fifty chance. I'm sorry. Did he like the—what was it I got him?"

"An MP3 player, and yes, he loves it. That was very nice of you, Richard." She sat down on the chair beside his desk and took a deep breath, then went for it. "Richard, we have to talk."

He took off his computer glasses and ran a hand through his hair. That meant he was flustered, at a loss for words. She knew him so well, liked and admired and even loved him. But she wasn't in love with him.

"This is about my proposition, isn't it?"

Elizabeth smiled. "I had thought of it as a proposal, but yes, I guess you could say that."

Richard's expression was almost comical. "Did I say proposition? God, that's pitiful. I'm sorry."

"No need to be sorry. It was a very nice proposition."

"It was a very selfish proposition. You're the best assistant I've ever had, and I didn't want to lose you. I thought it very sane, very sensible. We're compatible, and your boys would have anything you wanted them to have. And I'd have your fine mind, and your easy acceptance of my many foibles. It seemed to be win-win. Or, as Napoleon said on his way back from Moscow, it seemed a good idea at the time."

"I think, since you had me look it up, it was more like *from the sublime to the ridiculous is but a step.*"

"True. But, either way, it was a disaster of an idea, wasn't it?"

"No, Richard, it wasn't a disaster of an idea. In fact, besides being extremely flattered, I think you made me look at my life, which is something I hadn't done in a long, long time. That examination has made me realize that settling isn't something I want to do."

Richard sat forward on his desk chair, propping his chin in his hands. "Can we back up here a minute? I thought I was taking advantage of you bringing up the subject in order to let you down easy, but suddenly I'm not so sure. You're dumping *me?*"

For the first time since she met Will Hollingswood, Elizabeth felt relaxed in Richard's company. "I think we're dumping each other."

"You know about Eve," Richard said, sighing. "Elizabeth, I don't know how it happened…"

"I do. Eve's rather…irresistible."

Richard blushed. He actually blushed. "She told me her mother had warned her that when she got married it should be the first time for love, the second time for money. For the third time, Eve says she's willing to settle for great monkey sex. Oh, God, I shouldn't have said that. Not when we're in the middle of dumping each other. Still, I really wish we could be writing this down. It's great dialogue if I ever decide to write a wacky romantic comedy."

"Oh, I'm not so sure about—you're getting married?" Elizabeth was instantly concerned. "Richard, you barely know Eve."

"I don't know about that," he said, still looking sheepish, which was a rare but rather good look on him. "I think I met her several times in my more interesting dreams when I was about twenty-five years younger. I just didn't think women like Eve actually existed outside of fiction."

Elizabeth had to cover her mouth to conceal her amusement.

"No, don't smile. I'm being deadly serious here. I thought Jake LaRue was brilliant, a real man of the world. Turns out, he's an ass. *I'm* an ass. Cynical, superficial, selfish—pick any two of the three. I can't believe that not two weeks ago I thought my proposition— proposal—to you was exactly what was best for both of us. I'll be forty-six next January. I didn't think I should expect anything more than a comfortable relationship at this point in my life. Then Eve showed up and—well, I've been avoiding this talk since the day I met Eve, but now I realize that you aren't upset. You're relieved." His puzzled expression was rather comical. "Why?"

Elizabeth reached out across the desk and took his hand in hers. Holding his hand was a comforting feeling. It was the big, warm hand of a very dear friend. "It turns out you're not the only one who realized there's more to life than settling for what's comfortable. I was dreading telling you, but now we can congratulate each other on lessons learned."

"Will Hollingswood, right? He's more than the boys' soccer coach?"

"Baseball coach. No wonder you named Sam The Dog the way you did—how else would you remember who and what he is. But, yes, it's Will. I don't know where we're going, even if we're going anywhere, but he made me realize that my life didn't end when Jamie died. For a long time, I thought it had."

"You aren't leaving me, though, are you?"

She shook her head. "No, I'm not leaving you. I'd miss you terribly. I love my job. And I'd worry if you would remember to eat."

"You had to have been counting on the financial security I dangled in front of you. I can't forget that. I considered it to be my biggest bargaining chip, frankly. Let me set up college funds for the twins. It's the least I can do."

Elizabeth withdrew her hand. "Absolutely not, Richard. You don't owe me anything."

"Now I've insulted you. Very well, how about a raise? I believe I've already said that you're grossly underpaid."

"That's a deal," she told him, getting to her feet and giving him a kiss on the cheek. "Now, tell me what you're writing and hiding. I'm going to see it sooner or later, anyway."

Richard looked five years younger as his cheeks flushed in embarrassment. "I doubt that. It's an e-mail to Eve, and I'm fairly certain it's X-rated. Now, I thought you were on vacation. Go—vacation."

Elizabeth left the room while the going was good and didn't laugh out loud until she was on her way back to the boys. She hesitated at the bottom of the stairs, losing her smile as she realized that now that she and Richard were good again she had to tell Will what she had done.

"I don't have time to talk," Chessie said, quickly picking up a plastic-encased wedding gown and half hiding behind it. "See? Me, being busy. Very, very busy."

"Tough. I want to talk, and I need your advice," Will said, taking the gown from her and returning it to the hook on the wall of his cousin's office.

"Oh, all right, all right. Isn't it enough I spilled the beans about Elizabeth and her employer? God, I still can't believe I did that. I'm always so good with secrets. But you had me *so* mad…"

"Chessie, will you for God's sake just *sit?* It's all right, really. It doesn't matter that you set us up. It doesn't matter that she might have been using me for…well, for comparison, or something. I don't care about any of that. I really don't. I love Elizabeth."

That last admission seemed to do the trick, as Chessie all but fell into the chair behind her desk. "You *what* Elizabeth? Oh, this is bad. I know I just had a birthday last month, but I didn't think I was ancient enough to be needing a hearing aid."

Will pulled up a chair in front of the desk and sat down. "Can you be serious, just for one lousy moment?

Elizabeth is avoiding me. I know why. She's working through some stuff about her late husband, and that's okay, that's good, and it's probably very necessary. And she has to tell Richard that she doesn't want to take him up on his proposal. Of course, now that Eve is in the mix, I don't know that this is going to be too hard. The third thing, the thing I want to spare her, is that Elizabeth has to think she needs to tell me."

Chessie frowned. "Needs to tell you what?"

"Try to follow along, Chess. She has to believe she needs to tell me that she only went out with me to see if there was, well, hell, more out there than Richard."

"Actually, if we're being precise here, Counselor, that part was my idea. I sicced you on her, remember? So blame me."

"Yes, that was pretty much my plan," he said, then watched her reaction.

"Ha-ha, very funny." Then she frowned. "Wait a minute. Why is anybody blaming anyone? It all worked out, right? I've even got the wedding gown set aside."

"Excuse me? Wedding gown?" Will wasn't sure he was ready to hear this one.

"Oh, boy. I didn't think you were capable of a deer-in-headlights look, but you're doing a pretty good imitation. You don't want to marry her?"

"Chessie, we've known each other for less than two weeks."

"Yeah," his cousin said, grinning. "Next date, you might kiss her good-night, even make a try for second base. Come on, Will, get real. Elizabeth and I do talk, you know. You're no kid anymore and neither is she. Either you know by now or you wouldn't be here, trying to get me to do your dirty work for you."

Ah, he still had it, the great negotiating mind of a true defense Counselor, one who was currently defending himself. "Then you'll do it? You'll tell her there's no need for some big confession from either of us. That it doesn't matter how we got where we are, but just that we got…well, that we got there."

"You're pathetic," Chessie told him, shaking her head. "Correction, all men are pathetic. Turn around, Romeo. I want to see the big yellow streak going down the back of that designer suit."

"Now who's being a comedian," Will said, shifting uncomfortably in the chair. "I just don't see the need for any great postmortem of how something happened, why it started. Isn't it enough that we're where we are now?"

Chessie leaned her chin into her cupped palm. "Fascinating. This is absolutely fascinating. Is this anything like telling one of your clients not to answer a question unless it's asked, and not to ever volunteer to fill in any details? Of course, most of your clients are guilty as sin, so that might figure in there somewhere."

"Thanks for that rousing endorsement of my choice of profession," Will said, getting to his feet. "You said you're busy, so I'll leave now."

"Oh, sit down, you big crybaby," she ordered. "I'll help you. I mean, I can't take the credit for getting you two together if how I got you two together rips you apart now, right?"

His back to her, Will smiled and resisted a quick fist pump of victory.

"Thanks, Chess."

"Yeah, well, before you go ordering me a couple dozen roses to thank me—I like yellow ones, by the way—convince me that you're not going to hurt her. Because then I'd have to kill you, and you're my favorite cousin."

"You'll tell her, although I kept seeing her because I wanted to, that I originally asked her out because I owed you one for that last blind date I set you up on?"

"The last *three* dates you set me up on. Stick with the facts, Counselor."

"All right, the last three dates. But Bob Irving wasn't so bad, was he?"

"I'd rather have a root canal," Chessie told him evenly. "Two root canals."

"Point taken. No more setups, no more blind dates."

"Ah, there is a God. What else am I supposed to tell her? Should I be taking notes here?"

"No, I think you can remember that I only agreed under duress, and that it was you who spilled the beans to me about Richard Halstead."

"Keep it up, Will. Soon you'll be accusing me of doing away with Jimmy Hoffer."

"That's Jimmy Hoffa, and you still probably don't know who you're talking about."

Chessie shrugged. "I heard it somewhere. He's supposedly buried in some ballpark."

"The Meadowlands, which is a sports stadium. And stop stalling."

"But I like stalling. I can't believe I've agreed to run interference for you. Why am I doing this again?"

"Oh, I don't know, Chess. Maybe because you started it all?" Will suggested, tongue-in-cheek.

"Oh. Right. So I tell her I sicced you on her—to be platonic, if I recall correctly, which you probably bungled immediately. I tell her I let it slip that she was considering marrying Eve's new squeeze—can you believe that one? I mean, our own Eve and a big-time best-selling—"

"Uh-uh, back on point, Chess. You're almost done."

She stuck out her tongue at him. "I thought I was done. Or do you want me to tell her that business about you loving her? Do I look like Cyrano De Bergerac to you?"

"Only maybe a little, around the nose…"

He ducked as Chessie whipped a white satin ring bearer's pillow at him. He caught it deftly and then held it, looked at it. "Chess? You're the expert. Can you have two ring bearers?"

His cousin looked at him for a long time, her eyes taking on a rather moist, dreamy look. "You mean it, don't you? You really love her. Oh, Will…"

"Hey, don't get sloppy on me now," Will protested, laughing, as she came around the desk and flung her arms around him. Good old Chess. She deserved a happy ending of her own.

"So we're good?"

Elizabeth looked at Will as he handed their tickets

in at the gate, the boys already running ahead of them toward, naturally, the nearby cotton-candy booth. It was really their first chance to talk, as Mikey and Danny had pretty much monopolized the conversation all the way to the ballpark.

"I'm still rather embarrassed, but yes, we're good. Chessie took total blame for everything."

"I sent her three dozen yellow roses."

Elizabeth bit back a smile. "Yes, she told me. Apropos of nothing much, I guess, Richard gave me a raise."

Will put his arm around her shoulders as they joined the boys. "We could pretend this is our first date. Our first, nonengineered by someone else date? Except that would be rather pointless, don't you think? I'm just glad we didn't have to go through some tortured two-way explanations. So much easier to blame Chessie."

"I think she enjoyed explaining. She said she felt like she was back in high school. And I'll admit it, I'm glad we don't have to talk about any of it anymore."

"I've missed you, by the way."

She waited until he'd paid for two bags of instant tooth decay, and the boys headed for their seats as if they knew just where they were going, which they probably did. The male of the species had good memories for these things. "We've seen each other every day, at baseball practice, when you come to visit the boys."

Will pulled her closer for a moment, pressing a kiss against her temple. "Don't tell me you need me to draw you a diagram," he said teasingly.

"Well, maybe it was a good idea to…you know. Slow down for a while?"

"Maybe. But I would like to submit for the record that slowing down was not *my* idea."

He steered her toward the cement steps leading down to his reserved seats. Before she went ahead of him she dared to put her hand on his cheek and say quietly, "For the record, it wasn't my idea, either. But Mikey wasn't sleeping too soundly there for a while."

"Sure, blame the kid," Will whispered back to her, also giving her a quick swat on the backside, so that she laughed and hastened to her seat.

Elizabeth had been shocked, to say the least, when Chessie had asked her to meet her for lunch two days ago and told her that Will knew all about Richard's proposal and the fact that Elizabeth had been seriously considering it. Considering it to the point of going to Second Chance Bridal, trying on a wedding gown.

"Which I've got put aside for you, by the way," Chessie had told her. "No pressure, but you'll never find anything better suited to you. Now all you need is a groom, right? Should be a snap."

Not so much as a single serious boyfriend until Jamie, five years a widow, and suddenly Elizabeth might have to consider a second marriage proposal in a little more than two weeks?

Was it any wonder just looking at the twins downing their cotton candy by the handful was making her stomach queasy?

"Hot dog?" Will asked her.

"No! I mean, that is…no, thank you, I'm not hungry," she answered, feeling her face growing hot. "Did you hear about the big trade this morning?"

Will looked at her in some astonishment. "You know about the trade?"

She returned his look with one that said *doesn't everyone?* "We read the sports page every morning now at breakfast. The boys are improving their reading skills while thinking they're only having fun, and I'm learning more about baseball. Bringing a pitcher over from the American League should work well, at least the first time other National League teams face him, but I don't know if he was worth four of our IronPigs. We're supposed to be the top Phillies farm team, bringing our own talent up through the system, not a candy store for other teams to go shopping in when we want a new left-hander to beef up our bullpen."

"Good God, I've created a monster." He gave the bill of her pink IronPigs baseball hat a tap.

"Yes, I think you have," she said, rather pleased with herself. Then, emboldened, she added, "I sent Chessie a box of dark chocolate-covered caramels. Eve told me they're her favorite. I was so nervous about having to tell you about Richard. So, yes, I guess I was sort of avoiding you, even when you were visiting the boys. Then again, it wasn't until she told me she'd told you she'd pretty much tried to set you up as a sort of guinea pig that I really realized how…tacky the whole thing could be, if you didn't see the humor in all of it."

"There was humor in all of it? Would that be before or after I took you to bed?"

Elizabeth shot a quick look toward the twins, but they were busy watching the team mascots, a pair of huge plush pigs, chase each other around the infield.

"Maybe we shouldn't talk about this anymore," she said quietly.

"That was my idea all along. Yet here we are, talking about it. But I think I know what's still needed before we can just forget how and why we met, and concentrate on how we are now."

"Oh, and what's that?"

He took her hand and brought it to his lips, kissed her palm. "Elizabeth, I'm sorry. I set out to flirt with you on orders from my cousin, and I didn't let you know I knew when I found out about Richard. Now you."

Elizabeth took a deep breath, let it out slowly, even as she tried not to look as pleased as she felt. "All right. Apology accepted."

"And…?" Will prompted when she turned toward the field, to watch FeRROUS and FeFe Pig dance to the music now blaring out of the loudspeakers.

"Hmm?" Elizabeth looked at Will, eyebrows raised in question. "Was there something else?"

"You're not going to apologize for using me as a guinea pig?"

Elizabeth frowned, as if considering the question. Her heart was beating faster now, and she might even be hungry. Being with Will was so much fun, especially when he made her feel so alive, so *female.* "Nope. You made the first move, remember?"

"Okay, I'll give you that one. But what about not telling me about Richard?"

She shrugged her shoulders, then nodded her agreement. "But," she added, "exactly when was I supposed to tell you that Richard had asked me to marry him but I hadn't said yes yet? It's not the sort of thing that comes up much in conversation, you know? Besides, it wasn't as if you had asked me to move in with you or marry you or anything. You didn't even ask me to go steady with you, which was high school speak for being exclusive in my hometown, so what did it matter? Chessie explained it all to me. The whole thing was awkward, yes, but I was totally blameless."

"Remind me to kill that woman," Will grumbled as everyone in the ballpark stood for the national anthem.

By the seventh inning, Elizabeth had managed to down two slices of pizza and a tall cold soda, and the boys—and she included Will in that description—had consumed hot dogs, a large bag of peanuts and cups of colorful little frozen dots that turned to ice cream in their mouths. Elizabeth knew this because Mikey kept opening his mouth after taking a spoonful, to show her this grand metamorphosis.

It was a good thing she kept no candy or sweets in the house, although Elsie spoiled them with her home baking more often than Elizabeth could like. Still, a ballpark was a ballpark, and what was a ballpark without hot dogs and cotton candy and...and turkey legs.

Danny was sitting on Will's lap now, listening intently as Will pointed out the reason the outfielders shifted their positions depending on whether there was a right-handed or left-handed batter at the plate, while Mikey, who still tired easily, leaned his head against Elizabeth, who had put her arm protectively around his shoulder.

"Maybe we should cut this short," she said to Will. "We're up eight-to-two, and Mikey's running out of steam."

You'd have thought she'd asked the man to forego Christmas.

"No, the boys want to stay," Will said, so quickly it was as if he was verbally biting her head off. "Dan, Mike—you don't want to go home yet, do you?"

"I'm tired," Mikey said and then put a hand to his belly and looked up at Elizabeth with those big eyes of his, a trick he'd quickly learned got him her full attention these days.

"I'm not," Danny said, glaring at his brother. "FeRROUS and FeFe are going to shoot T-shirts at us from those little cannons before the Pigs come up to bat next time. Aren't they, Coach?"

"During the seventh inning stretch, right," Will agreed, patting Danny's back as if the child had just answered the bonus round question on some TV game show. "Why don't we do that, Mike? Stay for just this half-inning and the show, and then we'll get you home?"

"I think we should go now," Elizabeth whispered to

him, not understanding why Will seemed so adamant to stay. In fact, he looked almost desperate that they stay, and she might not have known Will all that long, but she'd never seen him look even remotely desperate.

"Okay," Mikey said, yawning. "But I'm still an inbalid."

"That's invalid, and you are not. The doctor said you're doing just fine." *And I should stop babying him,* Elizabeth told herself. "All right, Will, we'll stay."

"Was I overstepping some line here, Elizabeth? Coming between you and the boys?"

She shook her head. "No, not at all. I've been in charge for a long time, that's all. And sometimes when one of them says jump, I just ask how high. I'm overprotective, and it's got to stop. They aren't babies anymore, much as I want them to be. It's not going to kill Mikey to wait a few more minutes so that Danny can see the mascots again."

"You're not overprotective. You're a mommy. But you're right. Mike was just pulling your chain. Brings back memories of my younger days. Poor Mom, I could wrap her around my finger anytime I wanted to. I guess girls can do the same magic with their fathers. That's something to think about."

Elizabeth looked at him questioningly, but just then the batter for the Louisville Bats hit into a double play and the inning was over.

"Here comes FeRROUS!" Danny shouted, slipping off Will's lap, his hands outstretched and ready to catch one of the rolled-up T-shirts that would soon be launched into the crowd. Mikey was beside him in an instant, stepping all over Elizabeth's toes, his tiredness and crankiness of a few moments ago seemingly forgotten.

"And there's FeFe!" Mikey yelled, pointing down toward the infield. "What's FeRROUS got?"

"I don't know," Elizabeth said as the two mascots came together, taking hold of a large rolled up something-or-other FeRROUS had brought onto the field.

FeFe pointed in their direction, and the two mascots danced their way toward the seats as they separated, unrolling a long white banner with red letters on it.

"Oh," Elizabeth said, staring at the words.

Dan and Mike—may I please marry your mother?

"Oh," she said again as the boys began pointing to the animated screen deep in center field and she saw herself, saw all of them, live on the screen.

"What's it say? What's it say?" Mikey asked excitedly. "Look—there we are! We're up on the big screen!"

"Somebody wants to marry Mom," Danny said as Elizabeth felt every pair of eyes in the entire ballpark turning toward them expectantly.

"I do, boys," Will said, ruffling their curly heads. "Would that be all right with you? After all, you're the men of the household."

The twins exchanged looks, and then shrugged— mirror images of each other, as they so often were.

"Sure," Danny said. "It's okay with me. Mikey?"

Elizabeth looked to her son, only two minutes

younger than Danny, but several months behind him in many ways. She knew that would even out in time, but for now, Mikey always seemed to need her more than Danny did.

"Mom?" Mikey asked as the lady in the row just below theirs pulled out her phone and began taking pictures of them with it. "I guess it's okay. Is that okay with you?"

"Uh, here's where I take over, now that I have your blessing," Will said, and the next thing Elizabeth knew he was down on one knee. Vaguely she could hear peanut shells crackling. "Elizabeth, I love you all so very much. I know we haven't known each other very long, but the rest of our lifetimes won't be enough to show you how important you are to me, how much you and Dan and Mike have already enriched my life. Will you and your sons please marry me?"

Elizabeth looked around her, at all the people who seemed to be collectively holding their breath as Will's proposal played out on the big screen in center field.

"If I say no we'll have ruined everyone's evening, won't we?" she whispered to him as he got to his feet.

"If you say no, I'll have to move to Alaska and hide out in a cave," he told her, taking her hands in his. "Say yes, Elizabeth. I want to spend the rest of my life loving you."

A small smile began playing around the corners of her mouth. He was so sophisticated, so handsome…and such a loveable dope. "I'd miss you if you moved to Alaska."

"So it's a yes?" He really seemed worried.

"It's a yes," she told him, and then put her hands against his chest as he moved to kiss her. "But only because I love you. I love you with all my heart."

There was a lot of cheering going on as Will kissed her, but Elizabeth heard only her sons' simultaneous exclamations of "Oh, *yucky!*"

That is until the lady in the next row down exclaimed, "I got it! I got it all! I told you, Tom, this new phone would come in handy. Video *and* sound! Hey, you two want me to send you a copy?"

Epilogue

Exactly one month, three days and six hours after Elizabeth had walked into Second Chance Bridal and made a fool of herself by crying all over Chessie Burton, she was walking toward the rose-covered gazebo on Richard's estate, her hand on his arm as he hummed along with the string quartet he had managed to produce out of his magic bag of tricks.

Ahead of her, Chessie, dressed in a simple blue bridesmaid's gown that she'd confided had seen more than one wedding, but she still loved it, kept the pace purposely slow.

Danny and Mikey walked behind Chessie, each carrying a satin pillow heart, Elizabeth's wedding ring on one of them, Will's on the other. They were supposed to lead the small procession, but when Chessie suggested a dress rehearsal a few hours earlier it became clear that the boys thought "slow and measured" was a synonym for "full speed ahead."

They were so handsome, her boys, Jamie's boys. Although they knew their father only through photographs and the stories she told them about him, Will had made it clear that he would do his best in helping her raise her sons—but never at the expense of Jamie's memory.

For now the boys called him coach, but they'd come to her only this morning to point out that their friend Todd had a dad, and they'd like to have a dad, too, if that was all right with her. She'd kissed and hugged them both so hard they'd squirmed and asked her if she was going to cry.

Someday, maybe very soon, Will would hear himself be called dad by her two boys. Someday, not that far from now, maybe he'd hear other children call him da-da, then daddy, and then, "Hey, Dad, can I borrow the car?"

The walk across the lawn and along the aisle set up between the rows of white chairs continued.

Elizabeth's mother had flown to Allentown for the ceremony, and she was already dabbing at her eyes with her handkerchief, even as Eve stood beside her, patting her on the back while managing to wink at Richard.

Matt Peters, Will's best man and business partner, stepped down from the wide shallow steps of the gazebo to offer his arm to Chessie, and Elizabeth experienced a small shock when she saw a quite intense look swiftly come and go in Matt's eyes. Did Chessie know she had an admirer? It didn't seem so, as she'd flashed him the same happy smile she bestowed on everyone.

But then Elizabeth forgot Chessie, forgot Matt, forgot her mother, the boys, or even, for a moment, who she was…because Will had moved out from behind the wall of white trellis and red roses, and was walking toward her.

A man, not a nervous boy.

A woman, not a giddy girl barely out of her teens.

They were here to promise themselves to each other.

A promise, yes, but also a stunningly serious commitment, made not with wide-eyed dreams of happily ever after, but with full knowledge that there would be both good times and bad, joys and heartaches, triumphs and defeats.

"Here we are, Elizabeth," Will whispered to her after Richard had kissed her cheek and transferred her hand to Will's forearm. "The most beautiful woman in the world and the world's luckiest man. Are you ready for this?"

"I've never been so certain of anything in my life," she told him, a single tear running her cheek. "I love you so much."

She and Jamie had spoken their vows with smiles on their faces, firmly believing in the love and cherish part, barely concerned with the "until death do us part" that came at the end of those vows.

How little they had known, those two so deeply in love innocents. And maybe that had been a good thing. Would anyone dare to marry, dare to bring children into the world, if they were to first consider everything that could go wrong?

Yes, she told herself as she gazed at Will. *People would. She and Will would. People did it every day. Because more than anything else, they loved each other. And love was the best reason, the only right reason....*

* * * * *

*Don't miss A BRIDE AFTER ALL,
the next book in Kasey Michaels's
SECOND CHANCE BRIDAL miniseries
available June 2010!*

*Harlequin Intrigue top author Delores Fossen
presents a brand-new series of
breathtaking romantic suspense!*
TEXAS MATERNITY: HOSTAGES
*The first installment available May 2010:
THE BABY'S GUARDIAN*

Shaw cursed and hooked his arm around Sabrina.

Despite the urgency that the deadly gunfire created, he tried to be careful with her, and he took the brunt of the fall when he pulled her to the ground. His shoulder hit hard, but he held on tight to his gun so that it wouldn't be jarred from his hand.

Shaw didn't stop there. He crawled over Sabrina, sheltering her pregnant belly with his body, and he came up ready to return fire.

This was obviously a situation he'd wanted to avoid at all cost. He didn't want his baby in the middle of a fight with these armed fugitives, but when they fired that shot, they'd left him no choice. Now, the trick was to get Sabrina safely out of there.

"Get down," someone on the SWAT team yelled from the roof of the adjacent building.

Shaw did. He dropped lower, covering Sabrina as best he could.

There was another shot, but this one came from a

rifleman on the SWAT team. Shaw didn't look up, but he heard the sound of glass being blown apart.

The shots continued, all coming from his men, which meant it might be time to try to get Sabrina to better cover. Shaw glanced at the front of the building.

So that Sabrina's pregnant belly wouldn't be smashed against the ground, Shaw eased off her and moved her to a sitting position so that her back was against the brick wall. They were close. Too close. And face-to-face.

He found himself staring right into those sea-green eyes.

How will Shaw get Sabrina out?
Follow the daring rescue and the heartbreaking
aftermath in THE BABY'S GUARDIAN
by Delores Fossen,
available May 2010 from Harlequin Intrigue.

Copyright © 2010 by Delores Fossen

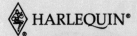

HARLEQUIN®

American ★ Romance®

LAURA MARIE ALTOM

The Baby Twins

Stephanie Olmstead has her hands full raising
her twin baby girls on her own. When she runs
into old friend Brady Flynn, she's shocked to find
herself suddenly attracted to the handsome airline
pilot! Will this flyboy be the perfect daddy—
or will he crash and burn?

Babies
&
Bachelors
USA

"LOVE, HOME & HAPPINESS"

www.eHarlequin.com

HAR75309

HARLEQUIN
Ambassadors

Want to share your passion for reading Harlequin® Books?

Become a Harlequin Ambassador!

Harlequin Ambassadors are a group of passionate and well-connected readers who are willing to share their joy of reading Harlequin® books with family and friends.

You'll be sent all the tools you need to spark great conversation, including free books!

All we ask is that you share the romance with your friends and family!

You'll also be invited to have a say in new book ideas and exchange opinions with women just like you!

To see if you qualify* to be a Harlequin Ambassador, please visit **www.HarlequinAmbassadors.com.**

*Please note that not everyone who applies to be a Harlequin Ambassador will qualify. For more information please visit www.HarlequinAmbassadors.com.

Thank you for your participation.

BAP09BPA

HARLEQUIN® *Presents*®

Bestselling Harlequin Presents® author

Lynne Graham

introduces

VIRGIN ON HER WEDDING NIGHT

Valente Lorenzatto never forgave Caroline Hales's abandonment of him at the altar. But now he's made millions and claimed his aristocratic Venetian birthright—and he's poised to get his revenge. He'll ruin Caroline's family by buying out their company and throwing them out of their mansion... unless she agrees to give him the wedding night she denied him five years ago....

**Available May 2010
from Harlequin Presents!**

www.eHarlequin.com

HP12915

◆ HARLEQUIN®

INTRIGUE®

BESTSELLING
HARLEQUIN INTRIGUE® AUTHOR

DELORES
FOSSEN

PRESENTS AN ALL-NEW
THRILLING TRILOGY

TEXAS MATERNITY:
HOSTAGES

When masked gunmen take over the maternity ward at a San Antonio hospital, local cops, FBI and the scared mothers can't figure out any possible motive. Before long, secrets are revealed, and a city that has been on edge since the siege began learns the truth behind the negotiations and must deal with the fallout.

LOOK FOR

THE BABY'S GUARDIAN, *May*
DEVASTATING DADDY, *June*
THE MOMMY MYSTERY, *July*

www.eHarlequin.com

HI69472

Love Inspired®

Former bad boy Sloan Hawkins is back in
Redemption, Oklahoma, to help keep his aunt's
cherished garden thriving and to reconnect with the
girl he left behind, Annie Markham. But when he
discovers his secret child—and that single mother
Annie never stopped loving him—he's determined
that a wedding will take place in the garden
nurtured by faith and love.

REDEMPTION RIVER

Where healing flows...

Look for

The Wedding Garden
by Linda Goodnight

*Available May 2010
wherever you buy books.*

Steeple
Hill®
LI87595

www.SteepleHill.com

REQUEST YOUR FREE BOOKS!

2 FREE NOVELS PLUS 2 FREE GIFTS!

SPECIAL EDITION

Life, Love and Family!

YES! Please send me 2 FREE Silhouette® Special Edition® novels and my 2 FREE gifts (gifts are worth about $10). After receiving them, if I don't wish to receive any more books, I can return the shipping statement marked "cancel." If I don't cancel, I will receive 6 brand-new novels every month and be billed just $4.24 per book in the U.S. or $4.99 per book in Canada. That's a saving of 15% off the cover price! It's quite a bargain! Shipping and handling is just 50¢ per book.* I understand that accepting the 2 free books and gifts places me under no obligation to buy anything. I can always return a shipment and cancel at any time. Even if I never buy another book from Silhouette, the two free books and gifts are mine to keep forever.

235/335 SDN E5RG

Name _____ (PLEASE PRINT) _____

Address _____ Apt. # _____

City _____ State/Prov. _____ Zip/Postal Code _____

Signature (if under 18, a parent or guardian must sign) _____

Mail to the **Silhouette Reader Service:**
IN U.S.A.: P.O. Box 1867, Buffalo, NY 14240-1867
IN CANADA: P.O. Box 609, Fort Erie, Ontario L2A 5X3

Not valid for current subscribers to Silhouette Special Edition books.

Want to try two free books from another line?
Call 1-800-873-8635 or visit www.morefreebooks.com.

* Terms and prices subject to change without notice. Prices do not include applicable taxes. N.Y. residents add applicable sales tax. Canadian residents will be charged applicable provincial taxes and GST. Offer not valid in Quebec. This offer is limited to one order per household. All orders subject to approval. Credit or debit balances in a customer's account(s) may be offset by any other outstanding balance owed by or to the customer. Please allow 4 to 6 weeks for delivery. Offer available while quantities last.

Your Privacy: Silhouette is committed to protecting your privacy. Our Privacy Policy is available online at www.eHarlequin.com or upon request from the Reader Service. From time to time we make our lists of customers available to reputable third parties who may have a product or service of interest to you. If you would prefer we not share your name and address, please check here. ☐

Help us get it right—We strive for accurate, respectful and relevant communications. To clarify or modify your communication preferences, visit us at www.ReaderService.com/consumerschoice.

S5E10R